I'm Always By Your Side: A Milwaukee Love Story

By: Sylvannah

To my beautiful friend Domonique ♡
You have supported all of my
endeavors since the beginning.
Thank you for being a great
friend, grammar checker, listener,
and a comedian when needed.
I couldn't ask for a better big
sister!   Love you lots!

Acknowledgements

First and foremost, thank you Father for blessing me with this opportunity, I don't take it for granted. This debut novel is for my mother (Katrina) and everyone else who told me I could do it; you know who you are. Thank you for your continued support and encouragement. I hope I made you all proud.

~Sylvannah

Chapter One

Brianna

    Pacing back and forth in the living room of our apartment, I became more and more upset with every step. The angrier I became, the harder I stomped across the oak wood floors; sure to scratch them with every step of my stiletto heels. My breathing was labored, my anxiety at an all-time high. A million thoughts running through my mind, all leading up to one question, "How could he do this to me?" I glanced at the breakfast nook, separating the kitchen from the living room area. The kitchen we made love countless times on the granite countertops that I picked out and cooked dinner together Friday nights. The breakfast nook that held my freshly made coffee each morning with light cream and four sugars, just the way I liked it; now held three empty Magnum wrappers.

    I walked over and picked up the condom wrappers. I counted them for the fourth time. Why? I don't know. Maybe I thought if I kept counting them, they would disappear. I had to touch them again to make sure they were real. And sure as shit, they were as real as the two-carat diamond engagement ring that rested right next to them.

    I felt my body temperature rise and was sure that steam was rising from my head. I slammed the condom wrappers back down on the breakfast nook, and retreated to the bedroom that my now, ex-fiancé and I will no longer share. On the way to the room, I contemplated damaging the place. Breaking the pictures that hung on the walls that captured a moment in time when everything was perfect between us. Looking at the pictures, it would have never crossed my mind that the man I love would disrespect me this way, again.

Kevin has cheated in the past, but over the last year, he has spent his time convincing me that it would never happen again. I thought for sure it was official when he asked me to marry him. However, he has never brought another woman in our home, has he? What type of man brings a woman to a home he shares with the woman he declared his undying love? The same woman whose father he asked permission to marry. I stood still, in the hallway, looking at the pictures that captured all of our happy moments. Pictures from our first date, anniversaries, holiday photos; all hung on the wall leading to our bedroom. The same pictures he and his bitch disregarded, as they made their way to our bed.

What kind of woman comes to man's home, a home that he shares with his *fiancée*, sees the pictures of history with her, their happiness; and yet still, stays and fucks him, *in my bed*? At that moment, I wanted to rip every picture on that wall down, break every frame, and tear every photo. But I didn't. Instead, I continued my march to the room to pack my shit, contemplating whether or not to burn the place down on my way out.

I went to the foot of the bed where my suitcase rested, still packed from my business trip. I opened it up and moved some things around, to make room for more clothes. I headed to the dresser and grabbed as many clothes as I could and stuffed them in the suitcase. Then, I went to the closet and grabbed two more suitcases and a duffle bag, and filled them with business suits and other clothes that were hanging. I proceeded to the master bathroom, grabbed the contents on my vanity and dumped them into a duffle bag, along with the jewelry box that sat upon the dresser.

I reserved the biggest suitcase for my most prized possessions, my shoes. I packed as many pairs as I could get into the oversized suitcase, and a few more in the duffle bag. I looked around the room to do one last scan for any essentials I may I have missed. Once I was satisfied, I took the suitcases and the large duffle bag one by one to my SUV. Once everything was packed, I came back into the apartment. I took a look around and thoughts of the times we shared together flooded my memory. Tears came to my eyes as I removed the keys to the apartment and his spare car keys, and placed them next to the two-carat diamond engagement ring and the empty Magnum wrappers. I turned to walk out the door, no longer mad or angry. I was a Williams' sister, and we didn't get mad, we got even.

***

"He did what!" my little sister yelled as I ran her the details of what happened this evening. With the pain of betrayal in my heart, a throbbing headache, and an SUV packed with suitcases of clothes and shoes; I ended up at the house that my parents gave my sisters and me before they retired and moved to California. It was my sisters' and I safe haven. The only stipulation my parents had, was no boyfriends could move in. The house was strictly for their daughters only. I was a sophomore in college when our parents moved to Cali, my oldest sister had just graduated from college, and my baby sister was starting her first semester.

We decided to stay at home as opposed to racking up student loans to live on campus, which meant we always had our boyfriends around, but none of them ever moved in. My oldest sister and I moved out after we graduated from college. My youngest sister still dwelled in the family house, with no intention of moving out any time soon. I was happy to see that she still upheld the rules.

While she ranted and raved about what she wanted to do to Kevin, how she would kill him, where she would hide the body, and who would be her alibi; I looked around the room and instantly missed my mother. She would know what to do in this situation. She always knew what to do. She always had an answer to my sisters' and my problems, especially when it came to men. I wanted to call her, but I didn't want to disrupt her with my problems. Plus, I knew Daddy would want to hop on the next plane and help my sister with her plan to kill my now, EX fiancé.

My thoughts were interrupted by a loud bang, preceded by my big sister marching through the front door. She immediately came over to me and gave me the biggest hug, just like mama would do. I lost all control over my emotions and began to sob like a baby fresh out of his mother's womb. My chest heaved in and out, the tears came rushing down faster than Niagara Falls.

I felt my baby sister join in on the hug, and I could hear her saying, "Bri, we can go over there right now and fuck him up if you want us to, just say the word." I continued to cry uncontrollably, I felt as though I couldn't breathe and no words would come out of my mouth. I felt my chest getting tighter and all I could think was that it was from my heart cracking and breaking into a thousand little pieces.

"It's gone be ok Bri, I promise," my big sister said.

She got up to grab some tissues out the box that rested on the coffee table. Apparently, my little sister, Bianca, was well prepared for my meltdown. I looked up after wiping my tears and saw she had a box of tissues, a bottle of wine, and three wine glasses waiting to do their part in piecing my life back together. I was so grateful for my sisters. They were always there for me when I needed them; we've always been very close, even as kids, which was rare. Our parents instilled in us at a very young age that we were to put each other first, that family was all we had.

I got up to go to the bathroom and wash my face, hoping some cool water would make me feel a little better and help me to collect myself. I was in rare form, I never cried, especially not over a man. But Kevin was different, or at least I thought he was. Never in a million years did I think he would cheat on me, again. I know that's so cliché, but it's true. Kevin and I had an understanding. If either of us got to the point where we were tempted or entertained the thought of cheating, we would break things off. Everything was going so perfectly. We had great communication, we were open and honest about our feelings, and we had great sex. He was my best friend. Now, it all seemed like a lie.

I sat in the bathroom on the edge of the tub, wondering where things went wrong. Thinking, *"Did I miss any signs or any warnings that he was going astray?"* Wondering, *"How long has this affair been going on? Who is the bitch that he fucked in our house, in our bed?"* We've been engaged less than three months! So many thoughts and feelings were running through my mind, I was unaware of how long I was in the bathroom, until I heard Brooke knocking at the door.

"Bri, you alright in there?" she asked.

"Yeah, I'm good, be out in a second," I responded

"Aye Bri, don't be in there swallowing pills and shit!" Bianca joked.

I couldn't be mad at her; she was trying to lighten the mood. Something we all did when things were tense; it must be a Williams' thing. I swung open the door to two beautiful dark faces with big brown eyes staring back at me. There was an awkward silence, before we all busted out laughing at Bianca's joke. I followed my sisters back to the living room where we popped open the bottle of wine and talked about how I could get back at Kevin. Like I said, we Williams' sisters don't get mad; we get even.

Bianca

I knew Kevin was a snake the moment I met him. Brianna brought him to a cookout we were having for the fourth of July. I tried to hook her up with one of my boo's friends, but she wasn't having it. She was stuck on stupid by Kevin's corny, controlling ass. I would say I didn't see why she was so into him, but I'd be lying. The brotha was fine! Average height, dark mocha colored skin, full lips, and a nice athletic build, but more on the heavier side, like a football player. He definitely had presence about him, and when she walked in the backyard with him on her arm, we all took notice. It wasn't until towards the end of the night when he started to show his true colors.

We were all seated around the deck carrying on our own individual conversations until Brooke, being the pain in the ass big sister she is, started playing twenty questions and shit. It was cool for a moment, but Kevin must have felt like she was putting him on the spot because after a few questions in, he made an excuse to go for a bathroom run. Our other sister, Kris, who's actually my oldest sister's BFF, showed him where the bathroom was, while we pressed Bri for details on Kevin. Kevin was gone for quite some time, and after pretty much determining my sister was dick whipped, I returned my focus back to my boo. When Kevin returned, he pretty much demanded that he and Bri leave and go to his place. Of course, I had something to say about it.

"Why y'all leaving so soon?" I asked.

Bri started to speak, but I cut her off to direct my question to Kevin, who was too busy starring at Brooke's ass to notice. When he saw me staring at him, he immediately straightened up and offered me some lames ass excuse about having to get up early for work. So I said, "Well you can leave, and Bri can stay. We will drop her off later."

"That's not gonna work for me," he said. Then turned to Bri and asked, "You ready?"

I started to interject, but a look from Brooke told me not to say a word. I walked over to Kris and ignored Bri as she said her goodbyes while she followed her Master out the yard.

I asked Kris, "Did you see the way he was staring at Brooke's ass? What a creep!"

"Was he? I didn't even notice," Kris said, and then walked off to join the others.

I knew right then that Kevin wasn't to be trusted. If a man will check out your *sister's* ass right in front of you, he was definitely a cheater. As Bri and Kevin's relationship progressed, Brooke and Kris became fond of him, but I never liked him. I just couldn't stand the fact that he could keep Bri from spending time with us and I hated even more, the fact that she would allow him to do it. She even missed this past year's Thanksgiving family dinner because he wanted her to cook at home. The longer they were together, the less of Bri we would see.

There was even a time when we invited Kevin to join us for a movie night with the girls, and he declined saying that he already made plans for him and Brianna. Come to find out, his plan was takeout and HBO. Hell, he could have done that with us! After seeing Bri put so much time, love, and effort into maintaining their relationship, it was hard seeing Bri broken like this. Kevin was gonna get his; believe that.

When Bri came out the bathroom, I had already decided that it was time to get her mind off Kevin and the best way to get over something old, was to get under someone new. I'm just saying that one bump in the road ain't gone never throw me off course. Fuck a nigga, they come a dime a dozen, that's my motto. I bet Kevin would get his act together if he knew he wasn't the only option. Hell, Matt, Brooke's husband, found out the hard way too. Like I said, Kevin will get his, but my first priority was my sister.

We all sat back down in the living on the couch, it was an awkward silence and the mood was bringing me down. I was hurting for my sister, and I was ready to kick Kevin's ass, then go out for drinks to celebrate.

"So Bri, we going over there or what? Daddy didn't teach us how to shoot for nothing; I bet he had this very situation in mind," I said, only half-joking.

"Hold on Mrs. Smith, ain't nobody shooting nobody, but we gone figure this thing out. What you wanna do Bri? Do you still want to be with him?" Brooke asked.

"And before you answer that, remember this his second time getting caught!" I added.

"No, I'm done making excuses for him," Brianna responded.

"Are you sure, because we can get him back. The same way we got Matthew to act right, I'm sure we can get Kevin to do the same," Brooke said.

"Yeah, but the only difference is, Matt was smart enough to keep his dick in his pants; Kevin wasn't," I responded.

Brianna

I listened to my sisters go back and forth about my situation. As I listened, I recalled Brooke and Matt's situation that almost cost them their relationship. Brooke's boyfriend, now husband, Matthew, was being a little too friendly with his co-worker. They never slept together, but it sure was leading up to it. Matthew and Brooke had just moved in together. Matthew works as an analyst at the bank and sometimes have to do some work from home. He left his laptop at work and needed to check his email, so he used Brooke's iPad. I guess he also checked his personal email and didn't close out of it, and Brooke happened across some emails from Matt's co-worker talking about a recent lunch date and some chatting and flirting back and forth. The killer part was the semi-nude pictures attached to one of the emails.

Brooke was so pissed; she called for a lunch date and told Bianca, Kris, and me everything that happened. Matt, didn't know that Brooke read the emails, so we were trying to come up with a plan to make Matt realize that he was, what me and my sisters like to call, "At Risk". He was at risk of losing everything, Brooke included. We decided that we would come up with a level five plan, yes, level five; we play no games when it comes to revenge.

We had our own personal scale of how devious payback should be and since they had not slept together, we decided to take it easy on him, but needed something good enough to wake his ass up. We decided to wait until Greek weekend to get even with him, since he would be out of town. We were all sorority women, including Kris, and we were hosting a picnic. It was open to everyone, Greeks and non-Greeks.

When we made it to the park, it was exactly as we expected, packed with lots of fraternity men and sorority women; but most importantly, men. It was a hot July day, so most of the men walked around shirtless showing off their brandings and fraternity tattoos. We immediately went into action, taking pictures of Brooke with every shirtless guy there. We had pictures of her chatting it up with different people, but we made sure that the Philly bred body of a God, Rashad, better known as "East Coast" to me and my sisters, was in every shot. We needed to keep our shots consistent for the reaction we needed. Once Kris decided she had enough shots, we enjoyed the cookout, and retreated to the house to finish executing our plan.

We uploaded all of Brooke's pictures to her Facebook page and tagged several people who happened to be in them. Of course, East Coast was one of them. Did I mention that Brooke wore her shortest pair of royal blue shorts, the ones that Matt loved to see her in when he was around, but hated for her to wear if she wasn't with him? Along with a halter shirt that cut low in the front to accentuate her double D breast and cut short above her belly to show off her belly ring. Matt was going to have a heart attack when he saw those pictures. As soon as the pictures were uploaded, comments started raining in; "Likes" for Brooke's photos were popping up, comments about how cute she looked from the women, and how sexy she looked from the men. Our plan was working perfectly.

That night, we waited around for Matt to call, and we didn't have to wait long. Matt, called and Brooke immediately put him on speakerphone.

"Hey love," she answered sweetly.

"Hey baby. So, how was your picnic? You have a good time?" he asked.

"Yes, I had a great time! I can't wait to meet up with everyone again tomorrow for the gala. You're still coming with me right?"

"Umm…yeah of course."

"Ok cool, so how's work?" Brooke asked, waiting for him to ask her about the photos.

"Work is work. I should've stayed home and went with you to that cookout. I see you had them short ass shorts on," he responded.

Bingo! Brooke thought. Now it was time to have some fun.

"Oh those. Baby, they're not that short." She laughed.

"Yes, the fuck they are. Brooke, you know I don't like you wearing them. And you got yo belly ring all out and shit." He was clearly pissed.

"Since when do you have a problem with the way I dress? You always liked those shorts and my belly ring." Brooke almost couldn't contain her laughter.

"Yeah, for me to see. I saw all them pictures with you all hugged up with different guys and guys staring at yo ass and shit. When I get home, they are going in the trash!" he responded.

Brooke started to get pissed, but it gave her pleasure knowing that she had him right where she wanted him. Our plan was working perfectly. Whenever Matt started cursing, he was clearly upset.

"Wait a minute, just like you should've gotten rid of them half naked pictures of that bitch you fucking at work?" Brooke responded, throwing all of us off guard. She told us he didn't fuck the girl. She must've read the looks on our faces, because she mouthed the words, "I just wanna see what he gone say."

Silence was on the other end of the phone.

"Hello? You ain't got shit to say now huh?" Brooke asked.

"Baby...I...I swear to God I didn't fuck her. It was only one lunch and some flirting here and there. That's all that it was, I promise. Damn, I'm so sorry baby. I fucked up...I-" Click. Brooke hung up the phone.

For the next thirty minutes, Matt tried calling back. After over twenty missed calls and thirteen text messages, he finally gave up.

The next day, Brooke and Matthew did not show up at the Black and White Gala. Brooke called us the following day and told us that Matthew came home and pleaded with her. She said that he even fucked her so good she damn near blacked out during her orgasm, her words, not mine. He cut off all communication with his co-worker that was non-work related and pledged to spend however long it took making up to Brooke because he did not want to lose her to one of those "bums" who was all over her at the cook out.

About six months later, Matthew and Brooke were engaged. I guess he was serious about not wanting to lose her. She told us that he said he just couldn't take seeing her in the arms of someone else. I guess that picture of her hugging East Coast took the cake. However, even as I think back now on her situation and how things worked out, I had no hope for Kevin and me. It was over; there was no excuse for what he did. No excuse at all.

I was snapped from my train of thought to the sound of my cellphone ringing. I thought I left it in the car, but I looked back and saw that my sisters had unloaded my SUV and all of my belongings were sitting neatly at the front door. I got up to get my phone out my purse and noticed it was Kevin calling. He must have made it home and saw the items I left for him on the breakfast nook. I didn't feel like talking to him, so I pressed decline. I came back to the couch where my sisters sat quietly watching my every move. I picked up my glass of wine and gulped it like it was a shot. I looked over to Bianca and asked, "You got anything stronger?"

"No, maybe we should go to a bar or something? Let's get out the house for a while. Are you up for it Bri?" she asked.

"I'm down, Matt's out of town for work. I think that's a good idea," Brooke said.

"Not really, but I need a real drink," I said.

We all piled into Brooke's car and headed to one of our favorite spots.

Kevin

This is Bri, leave a message at the beep, peace!

"Shit!" I yelled as I threw my phone on the couch. How could I get caught slippin like this? I should've known she would come home early from her trip. Something told me to send shorty packing last night. But what can I say? I'm a sucker for good head, and shorty was the best. I mean she's a *BEAST.* No gag reflexes, just deep, hungry and sloppy, just the way I like it. She knew how to get what she wanted from me and she knew it.

I told her it was time for her to bounce and she started whining and pouting, talking about wanting to be with a brotha, knowing damn well I had a woman, a good woman at that. My woman didn't play and would beat the breaks off shorty if she found out what we've been doing. Hell, she'll kill me too! Which was the first thought that came to my mind when I walked in the house and saw them damn condom wrappers on the counter. Not to mention, she gave me back her engagement ring. Shit was real, and I had no clue how to fix it.

I've been blowing up her phone and she keeps sending me to voicemail. I already know she done caught up with her sisters and told them what she found. *Fuck!* If I knew Bri, which I do, they were over there plotting to kill my ass, or close to it. I knew all about that bullshit they did to my boy Matt that was fucked up. I would've fucked dude up if I was Matt, the way he was all up on Brooke's ass.

I thought for a second about driving over there before she let all of our business out, but even I knew that wouldn't be a smart move. I would've had to slap the shit out of Bianca's old gangsta ass, that chick had a mouth on her and thought she was tough. I scratched that idea real quick. I needed to talk to Bri alone, but I just didn't know how I would do that if she wouldn't take my calls.

I thought about calling Brooke. We were cool, she's the oldest and always kept it real with me when it came to Bri and me, but I knew I had no wins. You know the saying, "Blood is thicker than water"? Well, nothing or nobody sticks together like those three, including they friend Kris. When you get all of them together and you might as well throw in the towel. But I had to talk to Bri, so I kept calling. Eventually, she would pick up.

Brianna

When we stepped into the small lounge, we immediately noticed our favorite bartender was on duty. I did a beeline for the bar, followed by Brooke, while Bianca headed straight for the small dance floor. She was always the more outgoing one of the three of us. She was also horrible at a crisis and avoided uncomfortable situations at all costs. I guess me being an emotional wreck was too much for her to handle at the house, at least here she could get distracted by the music and unlimited supply of alcohol. That was Bianca; she always liked to pretend that problems didn't exist. In her life, they didn't, at least not yet.

She hasn't had to deal with heartache, or anything major, especially when it came to men. She was always the heartbreaker. Never stayed in a relationship too long, and preferred to have relationships with no strings attached. I admired that about her. She was so uninhibited. Brooke and I were the opposite. Brooke married her first and only boyfriend, and I was a hopeless romantic. Always kissing a lot of frogs and experienced a lot of heartache, until I found the one. Or thought I did, but it turns out, I didn't.

I felt myself getting emotional, so I called over the bartender to order some shots. I turned my ringer off on the way to the lounge, but I kept checking my phone to see if Kevin was calling. I now had over twenty missed calls and three voicemails. While Lance the bartender was pouring our shots, I read one of the six text messages from Kevin.

Please talk to me, baby I can explain.

How can you explain three empty condom wrappers being on our bedroom floor? Kevin and I stopped using condoms over a year ago, when I got an IUD. I read the next message.

Baby, please. Just hear me out. Where are you?

I wanted to call him back and hear him out, but not tonight. Things would be said, that shouldn't be said. I couldn't help but think that if I hadn't come home a day early, I wouldn't have known and my life would be bliss again. I was about to read the next text, but as I scrolled another call from Kevin was coming through, and I unintentionally accepted the call.

"Hello...hello? B, you there?" Kevin kept calling out, but I had no words. I was mute. I tried speaking, but nothing came out. I ended the call. Immediately he called back, and I sent him straight to voicemail. I took my shot and told Brooke that I'd be right back. I needed to be alone, so I went to the restroom. Thankfully, no one was inside, so I locked the door behind me. My phone lit up, signaling that I had a new voicemail. I listened to all four of them.

"Umm Brianna, baby. Please call me back. It's not what it looks like. Just please let me explain".

"Baby, please come home. Let's talk this out. Remember that we said we would always talk

things out? Please give me a chance to explain. I love you baby."

"*Brianna, baby... I need you baby. Please don't go. Come home, please,"* he cried.

I thought, "Now *HE's* crying. Give me a break. What the hell is he crying for? He got what he wanted. I damn sure hope it was worth it."

I was so pissed off at this point, I didn't realize I was now pacing the bathroom floor, and thinking aloud. I stopped pacing when another call came through, Kevin. I pressed ignore. I took a deep breath ready to listen to the last call, when another voicemail came through. I listened to the first one.

"*Where the fuck are you Brianna?! Ok, fuck it then. If you don't wanna work this shit out, fuck it. Go ahead and party wherever the fuck you at! I hope you find what you looking for in the fucking club!*"

"No this asshole didn't!" I said aloud to myself. "Just like a fucking snake to try to turn the shit around."

I was so angry, I didn't want to listen to the last voicemail, and started to regret not setting his shit on fire before I left. I took some deep breathes to obtain my composure and listened to the last message.

"*Baby, I didn't mean that. I'm sorry. I just really need to talk to you. Please let's work this out.*"

I was angry. I was confused. How could this happen to me, I thought. I powered off my cell phone and left the restroom to find some peace in my good friend, Tequila.

Chapter Two

Brianna

I woke up the next morning with a throbbing headache. I opened my eyes and took in my surroundings. The sun was shining in through the large bay window and reflecting on the lilac colored walls. There was a chest beneath the window, with a cushioned lid, where a host of stuffed animals of various sizes rested on top. On the left side of the room, there was a large armoire with three large drawers on the bottom. On the right side of the room, was a small computer desk, a chair and a large walk-in closet. In front of the closet lay three suitcases and a large duffle bag. Suddenly, the events of last night came rushing back to me. It wasn't a bad dream; my relationship was over. I couldn't remember all of what happened last night after we arrived at the bar. The last thing I remember was listening to voicemails from Kevin, and him pissing me off.

I lay back down to gather my thoughts. I looked over at the nightstand next to my bed to find a digital alarm clock, a bottle of room temperature water, two Advil and some BC Powder. It was close to 10 AM. Church was out of the question, I knew Kevin would look for me there, and I wasn't in the mood to be around anyone other than my sisters. I took the BC Powder and drank the entire bottle of water, then turned back over, closed my eyes, and drifted back to sleep.

By the time I woke up again, it was after one o'clock. I got up and rolled out of bed, this time my headache had subsided, but I felt dehydrated. As I climbed out of the bed, I noticed I was still wearing the clothes I had on last night. I slid my skirt down, trying to smooth it out, and walked to my bedroom door. Before stepping out, I listened to see if my sisters were out of bed. Hearing nothing, I proceeded out the door and downstairs to the kitchen, for a bottle of cold water.

To my surprise, both Bianca and Brooke were already in the kitchen, probably talking about last night. When I walked in, they both stopped talking and just stared at me. You would have thought I had two heads the way they were looking at me.

"Good afternoon ladies," I said.

"Hey," they said in unison.

I guess they were waiting to feel me out, to see if I was still an emotional wreck. On the inside, I wanted to scream. I wanted to fall to the floor kicking and screaming, asking God, why me, but I did enough crying last night. Today, I wanted to be alone with my thoughts. Therefore, I ignored my sisters, grabbed my bottled water, and retreated to my room.

Once I was alone again, I shuffled through my purse to find my phone. I wanted to know if Kevin left any more messages. Part of me felt like if he did, it meant that he still cared. I saw that he had left me three more messages, two of which had been left this morning. I started to think that maybe, just maybe, we could work things out again. Maybe he did have a good reason to fuck some random bitch in our bed. However, that thought was quickly replaced by heartache, which was eventually replaced by rage. I had so many different emotions come over me that it was starting to physically drain me. I finished my bottle of water, without listening to any of the messages, laid back on the bed, and once again, sleep consumed me.

Brooke

"She looks awful, Bianca. What are we gonna do? I hate seeing her like this," I said.

Bianca and I were hanging out in the kitchen trying to come up with a way to get Brianna out of her funk. It was like last fall all over again, at least this time Brianna wasn't calling us from jail. Last year, Kevin's dirty ass cheated on Brianna with her trainer, some little Hispanic chick named Maria. Brianna found out she and Kevin had been texting back and forth.

One night Brianna followed Kevin when he said he was going to hang out with some friends, and ended up catching him meeting up with Maria at a hotel. Brianna camped out for hours waiting for them to come out, but got tired and went back home. The next day, she and Kevin went to the gym and she confronted both of them. Kevin, of course denied it, but I guess Maria didn't get the memo and told Brianna that Kevin was her man now and he didn't want Brianna anymore.

Big mistake, Brianna lost it. She and the girl Maria started fighting, and no one could break them up. Apparently, the fight broke out near the free weights area because Brianna got a hold of a five-pound metal dumbbell and hit Maria in the face with it, knocking her unconscious. The police was called and they took Brianna into custody and Maria to the hospital. Kevin also received a blow from Brianna that left a nasty gash above his eyebrow.

Brianna called me that night after being arrested and told me everything that happened. Since it was the weekend, she would have had to stay in jail until Monday, but one of Bianca's friends was able to pull some strings to get her released. I don't know what he did or how he did it, but Brianna never saw the inside of a courtroom and the incident was never on record. It was as if it never happened. She never heard from Maria again either.

As far as her and Kevin went, we thought for sure it was over, but somehow he eased his way back in. It wasn't that I liked Kevin, I just tolerated him because he made my little sister happy, but now, that all changed. He was gonna get what was coming to him. He sure did have us fooled though. I thought for sure after that slight concussion Bri gave him, she knocked some sense into him. He always seemed to be showing himself worthy this past year. The surprise engagement really convinced us; well I mean me, that he was a changed man. Bianca and Kris weren't convinced, but Bianca never liked him, and Kris was always bitter when she didn't have a man. I guess nothing is really what it seems though.

I turned to Bianca, "Matt comes home today. Do you think she will want to come over later for dinner, just to get out the house?" I asked my sister.

"I doubt it. She just need some time."

"Yeah, I feel you. Are you coming?"

"Nah, I got a date." She smiled

"Look at you. You need to settle down, with ya hot ass." I laughed.

"Whatever B." She laughed.

I started heading for the door. "I will catch y'all later. I need to get some things together before Matt gets home. Love you," I yelled.

"Love you more," Bianca responded. And I was out.

Brianna

I must have had Kevin on my brain because I had a dream about the night we shared right before the last time I caught him cheating on me. I almost caught a case over his ass. Last year around Thanksgiving, I was working with a trainer to get myself ready for our annual New Year's Eve party. Kevin and I were working out at the same gym and occasionally; we would go to the gym together. While I was training, Kevin would stick around and do his own thing.

Well this particular evening, I wasn't feeling well so I decided to stay home. I ended up dosing off on the couch and by the time I woke up Kevin was already home and in the shower. I walked into our bedroom and Kevin's phone was vibrating with a text message that came through. I looked at the name on the screen and saw that it was from Maria, my trainer.

I read the message, *"Thanks for the great workout, see you next week☺."* At first, I didn't trip because I took it for what it was, they were at the gym and they worked out together. Then, I realized that Maria had Kevin's number. I stormed in the bathroom and confronted Kevin.

"Why is Maria texting you? How did she get your number?" I asked.

"Why you checking my phone? Since when we do that?" he spit back.

"Just answer the damn question, Kevin," I yelled.

"Look B, we just worked out together. She came over and asked where you were, and I told her you was sick. Since I'm paying for the sessions whether you show up or not, I figured I might as well get my money's worth," he said getting out of the shower.

I just stared at him, the water dripping from his body slowly smothering the fire of anger that was burning inside of me. He was so damn sexy. I just wanted to lick the beads of water off his abs and broad shoulders. I snapped out of my trance as he reached for a towel and wrapped it around his waist. He proceeded to the bedroom and I was right on his heels.

"So, how did she get your number?" I asked.

"I gave it to her," he said nonchalantly

"You what?!" I yelled

"Calm down B. I only gave it to her because she wanted to list me as an emergency contact for you, in case something happened if I wasn't around."

"Yeah right, ok. I ain't gonna trip, but I am gonna tell her not to be texting you. That number is for emergencies only," I said, feeling defeated.

Kevin just stood there staring at me.
"What?" I asked.

"You look so damn sexy when you mad." He smiled

"Whatever," I said, as I tried to push passed him, but he grabbed me and kissed me.

I tried to pull away, not because I wanted to, but because I was still mad. He grabbed the back of my head forcing our kiss deeper and my pussy was instantly wet. I reached down for his towel and let it fall to the floor. He wrapped one arm around my waist and held me close, as he took his other hand and slid off my shorts revealing no panties, he smiled. I took his manhood into my hands and massaged it, squeezing it and rubbing it, while pre cum oozed onto my hands. Never breaking our kiss, I heard him release a muffled groan. With that, he picked me up and carried me to the bed.

As I lay back on the pillows, he softly kissed my neck and caressed my thighs. His hands moved up my waist taking my T-shirt up with him. He pulled the shirt over my head and threw it to the floor. Our tongues met again as his hands found their way back to my weakest points, one on my left breast caressing my nipple and the other between my thighs massaging my clit. Kevin always knew what would set me off. My stomach muscles started to get tight, I knew then that I was about to cum. Just when I was almost there, he stopped.

Confused, my clit throbbing, heart racing and out of breath, I looked over at Kevin to catch him grinning at me.

"Tell daddy how bad you want it," he said.

"Really bad, baby please? Don't stop," I whined.

He said, "Show me."

I lifted up off the bed and rolled over to where he was. I kissed him until he fell back onto the bed, and straddled him. I placed soft kisses down his neck as he grabbed my ass. I removed his hands from my ass and eased my way down to his chest. Kevin loved when I licked his nipples, so I made sure to pay each one special attention as I grinded on his dick. I slipped my hand down and grabbed is dick, and rubbed it against my clit as I licked his nipples. He released deep guttural moans that turned me on.

I proceeded south, to my favorite part of him, along the way gliding my tongue down his chest and across his abs. He was hard as a brick. I ran my tongue along the length of his shaft and I felt him grab hold of my dreads. I loved it when he pulled my hair. I took him into my hot wet mouth and did my best to take in all of him. I heard him let out a long hard breath and yell, "Fuck," as he gripped my hair tighter.

At first, I sucked lightly, rolling my tongue around his dick while he filled my mouth. He started moving his hips and gliding his dick in and out of my mouth. I locked my jaws around him tighter and began to suck harder. "Shit baby," he moaned. I slid my mouth to the tip of his dick and lightly licked the head as I stroked his shaft with my hand. When I tasted his pre cum, I knew he was ready.

I climbed on top of him and straddled his waist. He lifted me up with one hand around my waist and placed his dick inside me. As his nine and a half inches filled me up, I gasped for air. The fact that his dick curved slightly meant that he hit my g-spot every time. Every time we made love, it felt like the first time for me. He was so well endowed, that for the first few minutes I always had to acclimate myself to him. As I rocked back and forth and rolled my hips, I felt him pressing deeper and deeper into me. It felt so good that I started to get dizzy. I leaned forward and rested my head on his chest as I bounced my ass up and down, ramming his dick into my g-spot.

"Slow down baby, I don't want you to cum yet," he said.

He grabbed my waist on both sides to try to control my movements, but just the mere strength of his hands around my waist and the sounds of our moans sent me into an orgasmic fit. My legs began to tremble, I couldn't catch my breath, and I came so hard. I could feel my wetness running down our thighs. Kevin was always so turned on when I came. He lifted me up, never disconnecting us, and put me on my back. He dug deeper and deeper until I could no longer take it and began to scream his name.

I tried to muffle my moans by biting him on the shoulder, but that turned him on even more and he began to thrust harder and faster. I threw my head back against the pillow and closed my eyes tighter taking every thrust like a champ. I tightened and released my pussy muscles around him as he grinded deeper and deeper. I could tell he was on the verge of releasing, so I did my best to squeeze harder. Not wanting to cum yet, Kevin slid out of me, and threw both of my legs over his shoulder and sucked on my clit. I let out a loud moan, "Aaaahhh shit, baby. Shit. Yes, Kevin."

"Tell daddy you love him," Kevin demanded and proceeded to sticking his tongue inside my pussy.

I was lost in bliss. He smacked my ass and repeated, "Tell daddy you love him."

"I love you dadddyyyyy!!!" I screamed.

"Say it again," he demanded.

"I...love...you...dad...dyyy."

"Whose pussy is this, B?" he asked.

"It's yours daddy," I responded.

"That's right, so cum for daddy, baby," Kevin said, as he made his tongue tap dance on my clit.

It wasn't long before I gave him what he wanted. My juices overflowed leaving cum dripping from his goatee. He placed me back on the bed and gently slid inside me. I could tell he was turned on by the way he made me come so hard. That always excited him. He plunged deep inside me and I was determined to make him feel as good as I felt. I started to gently roll my hips beneath him. I caressed his back and lifted my head, so I could flick my tongue on his right nipple. I ran my hands down to his hard ass and squeezed, pushing him deeper inside me.

I began to contract and release my pussy muscles around his dick as he start pushing harder and faster. He was about to cum. He lifted one of my legs onto his shoulder with one hand and grabbed a handful of my dreads with the other. Again, he went deeper, harder, and faster. I held on tight to my man, relishing in the painful pleasure until he let out a loud moan. I continued to grind into him as another orgasmic wave sent shocks through my body, and we climaxed together. Kevin stroked a few more times and collapsed on top of me.

He whispered, "Damn, I love you, B."

"I love you too baby," I replied.

***

The next morning, I woke up wet, sweaty, horny and hungover. I missed Kevin, but I didn't want to. It's been this way for the last three days, having wet dreams about the nights Kevin and I shared together. I wanted to forget about Kevin, so I replaced him with Tequila. Tequila has become my new lover, my new friend. I knew that I could depend on him to calm my anxiety, and take me to a state of euphoric relief until I couldn't take anymore and I blacked out.

The first night I found out about Kevin's infidelity and I drank until I blacked out; I have to admit that it scared me. Now, it's a welcome escape from the real world. Each moment I woke up with a throbbing headache, hoping that memories of my heartache were erased along with memories of the previous night's events. But they weren't, in fact, they came rushing back the moment I opened my eyes and saw the missed calls on the lock screen of my iPhone.

I popped two Advil without water, and headed over to my unpacked suitcases. I was tired of sitting in the house hiding from my sisters and the rest of the world. It was time for me to get my life back on track. I have already missed three days of work. Brooke called my boss, told him that I was sick and dropped off the report I prepared from my conference. I wasn't ready to go back to work just yet. I had endless hours of sick time and vacation time to use, so after pulling out some running shorts, a t-shirt, sports bra, socks, and my running shoes, I called my job and told them that I need to take the next two weeks off for vacation. I explained to my boss that constantly working long days and late nights have finally caught up with me. He agreed that I needed a break and told me that everything in the office would be taken care of in my absence.

I hung up the phone and headed down the hall to the shower. I hadn't showered in days and was in desperate need of soap and water. I turned on the shower and undressed. As the steam slowly covered the mirror in the bathroom, I stood looking at myself. My locks needed to be tightened, I had bags under my eyes from all of the crying, and my eyes were red from a combination of alcohol and tears. However, I tried looking passed all of that. I started looking at my five foot three inch frame.

I was in shape from all of the running, nice double-D sized breasts, flat abs, thick thighs, curvy hips; I could put any girl on the cover of King Magazine to shame with my ass. So, what was the problem? I worked hard as the top Account Executive at my company. I always made sure Kevin had what he needed; he got dinner every night, unless I was away for work. We had sex almost every night, whenever he wanted it. I made sure he had a full stomach and empty nuts. So, where did I go wrong? These thoughts consumed me and as I stepped into the shower, I allowed my salty tears to blend with the hot cascading water.

The water was too hot, but I needed to feel the stings to let me know that I wasn't dying because I thought for sure, the way I was feeling had to be what death felt like. The tears kept coming no matter how hard I tried to stop them. I had to gain some kind of control, I told myself. I turned the knob on the cold water to cool the temperature and washed my hair. As I washed my locks, I came up with a plan to get back at Kevin. I didn't know exactly what I would do, but I had to come up with something. By the time I was done with my shower, I decided that I would meet Kevin and hear him out.

I stepped out of the shower and wrapped my hair up in a towel. I placed another towel around my body and proceeded to my room. Once I got there, I called my loctician and scheduled an appointment to get my hair done. I looked over at my running gear; I guess that would have to be put on hold. I searched my bags and found a pair of jeans and a white tank top. I searched my duffle bag and large suitcase of shoes for my white flats, but I could not find them. I must have left them at the apartment. I settled for my white flip-flops, threw my hair in a ponytail, grabbed my purse, phone and car keys and headed for the door.

When I got to the bottom of the stairs, Bianca was sitting on the couch watching TV. I walked past her to the kitchen to grab a bottle of water. I needed to rehydrate myself. Bianca walked in the kitchen with a shocked look on her face.

"I see someone finally showered." She laughed. "How are you feeling?"

"I'm ok, just a little dehydrated".

"Where are you going?"

"I got an appointment to get my hair done," I responded casually. Before she could ask me any more questions, I shot back, "Why you ain't at work?"

"Oh, I took the next two days off. Me and Josh going to Chicago for the weekend to check out Navy Pier. I can stay here if you need me to; I know that Brooke and Matt are going away for the weekend too. So, if you don't want to be by yourself, I will stay here," she said.

I know Bianca felt guilty about leaving me, but they had plans and lives of their own. I'm a big girl. I can be by myself. I assured Bianca that I was fine.

"No, I'm grown. I don't need a baby sitter, have fun and enjoy your weekend. I could use the time alone," I said.

"Ok, well you know to call me if you need anything. I mean anything; I will hit the highway right away if you need me," she promised.

"I know, but I'm good. I'm the big sister remember?" I said with a smile. "Look, I gotta get to this appointment. Call me and let me know you made it to the Chi safe, ok?" I said.

"Ok, you be safe too," she said.

I hugged my sister and made my way to the door to get to my appointment. On my way out the door, I checked my phone and saw that I had four text messages and two voicemails from Kevin. I deleted the messages and the voicemails without reading or listening to them. I had already decided that I would see him, but it was going to be on my terms. I would call him when I was ready. I hopped in my SUV, turned up my Fantasia CD, and let her single, "*Lose to Win*" take over my eardrums.

***

When I pulled up to the hair salon, I was happy to see that it was not packed. Maybe because it was Thursday, but that meant I didn't have to listen to other women's problems and be reminded of my own. I checked my face in the mirror for any telling signs of my distress. I still had small bags under my eyes, but for the most part, the redness was gone. The sadness was still there. I could see it, I felt it; I just hoped no one else picked up on it. I applied a light coating of lip-gloss to my lips and made my way into the salon.

"What's up Diva?" Roxy greeted me.

"What's up Rox, how you?"

"Girl, livin'," she replied.

Roxy has been doing my hair since I did the 'Big Chop', that was almost six years ago. She is the baddest natural hair stylist in the city. Getting an appointment with her was like applying for government assistance, her waiting list was ridiculous. Overtime we have become such good friends; I was able to get same day appointments when she could fit me in. I never really took advantage of that until now, but I'm sure she knew it was time for me to get tightened up; it's been a while since we've seen each other.

"So, what's new girlie?" she asked

"Oh nothing much," I lied. "Just working too much that's all. The same old shit on a different day."

"I feel you. How's Kevin? Y'all set a date yet?"

I felt my body tense when she said his name and I wondered if she noticed it. I didn't want to air my business to the whole shop, so naturally I played things off and lied.

"Not yet, it's been so busy with both of our work schedules and things going on. We haven't had time to sit down and discuss everything in depth, but you know that I got you. I'm gonna need you to hook me up. I can't be looking crazy at my own wedding." I responded.

"Oh girl please, you know I got you."

I was relieved that she didn't pick up on my uncomfortable silence. The rest of the time there, we made small talk about what's been going on at the shop. She filled me in on all of the clients' gossip; we talked a little about work, and her family. I tried my best to keep the conversations about her and everyone else, to avoid talking about Kevin and me. Two and a half hours later, I was done. I paid her and promised to call her later this week for drinks.

When I got to my car, I called Kevin. I needed to get this over with. The phone rang a few times and just when I was about to hang up, he answered sounding out of breath.

"Bri? Baby, hello?"

"Hey Kevin."

"Hey baby, I was hoping you were gonna call. I missed you and I…" Before he could finish his sentence, I cut him off.

"Look Kevin, we need to talk. Where are you?" I asked.

"I'm at the gym. I can leave now and meet you wherever, just say the word."

"Meet me at Lola's at seven, and don't be late," I said and hung up before he responded.

That left me feeling like I was in charge, and finally taking control. Now, all I needed was a "fuck you" dress and a pair of heels that would pierce his heart with every step I made. I headed to the mall to find a new outfit. By the time I got back home, I had been to four different malls. I had three dresses to choose from, four pairs of heels, and a selection of accessories to match either of the outfits I chose.

I had about three hours before my meeting with Kevin, so I decided to have a glass of wine, put my feet up, and relax. As I lay back on the couch drinking my wine, it hit me. I didn't know what I was going to say to Kevin. I didn't want to come off like the girls in the books I read and the movies I watched. I wasn't weak like them, I didn't want to cry and ask why he did what he did. I didn't want to shoot out a laundry list of things I did for him. My plan was to start off physical, let him see me. Let him see the woman he betrayed. In my mind, I pictured him looking at me and mentally comparing me to the bitch he fucked in our bed. I pictured him realizing that she couldn't compare to me at all.

In my mind, I pictured him looking at my locs, how I kept them neat and tight, admiring my face, my brown eyes, my complexion, natural, no makeup, my full lips, that he used to adore so much.

I imagined him taking in the sight of my breast and remembering how he loved to suck, kiss, and bite my nipples. How they felt in his hands when he grabbed them. I imagined that he would look at my hips and smile because he loved the fact that he could see my ass without making me turn around. I pictured him, adjusting his dress pants because his dick was too hard for comfort when he saw me standing in front of him sexy, smelling good, with my dress accentuating my curves in all the right places, and killer shoes.

That made me smile. The first part of my plan would be to make him want me, and to make him remember what he gave up. I laid back and closed my eyes, satisfied with part one of my payback. I enjoyed the peace and quiet in the house and my wine, until it was time for me to get up and get dressed.

Kevin

What part of the game is that? I thought to myself as I looked at the phone.

"She just hung up on me," I said aloud.

I'm not even gonna sweat it, I'm just gonna go home and get fitted for tonight. I knew she wouldn't stay away too long. That's my baby, but I'd be a fool to think that it was gonna be easy to get her back. Brianna is a sweet woman, but she's not dumb, and she can be evil as hell if she wanted to be, I got the scar to prove it. Which brings me to my next thought, what would I tell her about the condoms? I couldn't lie and say that they weren't mine; she knows I wouldn't let somebody else fuck in my bed. Maybe I'll spin it and use it to my advantage. *Yeah I cheated, but at least I used protection.* Nah, fuck that. Ain't no way she buying that. Shit! I knew I should have sent that bitch home. Now I don't know how I'm gonna get out of this. I went to the locker room grabbed my bag and headed to my car. I needed to get home and get ready for tonight. I wasn't gonna leave Lola's without my fiancée.

When I made it home, I took a quick shower and started pulling something out to wear tonight. I needed to make sure that I was right for when Bri saw me. I knew she couldn't resist me in my chocolate colored suit so I opted to wear that with a cream-colored shirt and crimson and cream colored tie. I figured, since I couldn't talk my way out of this one, I might as well try to take her mind off it by distracting her with my appearance, and fucking her until she forgot about it. At least that was the plan; we will see how it goes though.

I stepped into the bathroom to shave. I didn't have any hair, but I liked to make sure that my baldhead remained smooth to the touch. I made sure to spray on Bri's favorite cologne. I got dressed because I wanted to make a few stops before I headed to the restaurant. First, I had to make a call to do some damage control.

"Hey baby, I'm glad you called. Are we still on for tonight?" she asked.

"Hey, that's why I called. I can't get with you tonight; I'm meeting Brianna for dinner".

There was a moment of silence on the line. I figured she had to take a moment and let what I said sink in, but I didn't have time, I needed to get going. Plus, she knew what it was.

"Hello?" I said.

"Yeah, what's going on with Bri?" she asked.

"I guess I will find out when I meet up with her at Lola's. But I gotta go, and shorty, I can't rock with you like that anymore. It was good while it lasted, but I gotta get my fiancée back." And with that, I hung up, grabbed my keys and Bri's engagement ring off the breakfast nook and headed out the door.

My first stop was to a small florist downtown to pick up a bouquet of long stem roses. Bri loved fresh flowers. Then I headed over to the jeweler to get her ring cleaned. I wanted to make sure it shined like the day I bought it. When that was done, I headed over to the restaurant to wait on her. I made sure that I was early, so that she could see my commitment, plus I wanted to see the look on her face when she walked in to see me. I found a good seat at the bar and ordered a drink while I waited. My phone rang and I thought it was Bri, but it was shorty, probably looking for an argument. I answered the phone, "What?"

"What you mean what?"

"Just what I said, what?"

"So it's like that? Just fuck me right?"

"Look shorty, you know what it is, don't act like you don't. Bri's my woman, you know that."

"You wasn't worried about that when you was fucking me, now were you?"

"Even still, who did I propose to?"

Silence.

"Exactly. Bye shorty." And I hung up.

Chapter Three

Brianna

When I pulled up in front of Lola's, I was lucky enough to find a parking space right in front of the restaurant. Just as I was pulling up, a couple in a burgundy sedan was pulling out. I waited for them to exit and pulled right in. I took this as a sign that things were going to go my way tonight. However, I still couldn't shake the nervous feeling I had in the pit of my stomach. I kept thinking, *"What if?"* What if he revealed something to me tonight that I couldn't handle? What if he told me that he loved me, but wasn't in love with me anymore?

Then I thought of the voicemails he left me, it was obvious he still loved me, or at least cared. Then I thought, *"Wait a minute. Why do I care if he still loves me? He disrespected me in the worst way."* Soon, my nervousness grew to anger and humiliation and for a second, I almost put my truck in reverse and took off, but I had to face him eventually. Therefore, I put my big girl panties on, applied a coat of gloss to my lips, stepped out my truck, and headed for the restaurant doors.

A group of men was walking to the door at the same time, one of them, who had a hard time taking his eyes off my ass, reached out and opened the door for me.

"Thank you," I said.

"No problem, Gorgeous," he replied with a smile.

That smile nearly knocked me off my stilettos. He was drop dead gorgeous, dark chocolate skin, full thick lips, stood about 6 feet 2 inches, athletic build, and long dreads that somehow worked well for him. I usually don't go for brothers with hair as long as mine, but this brother had it going on and then some. I didn't mean to stare, but I was caught in a trance, only for a second. My moment was interrupted when I heard Kevin call my name from the bar. I broke our gaze with an embarrassed smile, and walked over to Kevin, making sure I kept a sway in my hips for the chocolate, dread headed Adonis. I wore a look to kill on my face for Kevin.

As I approached him, he stood as if he was going to hug me, probably wanting to send a message to the handsome man that caught my eye, but he couldn't be serious. I dismissed his approach and took to the bar stool next to him.

"Um…hey. These are for you," he said nervously as he handed me a bouquet of red roses.

"Thank you," I said, still wearing my scowl.

He shrugged it off and asked, "Did you have to park far?"

I knew he was trying to make small talk, but I wasn't in the mood. I also knew that he was dying to make a smart comment about me being a half hour late, but he wouldn't dare. Not under these circumstances.

"No, I parked out front," I responded.

"They said it will be about a thirty minute wait for a table. That was over thirty minutes ago, so we should be seated shortly," he said

Just then, a young blonde waiter came over to seat us. She was very pretty and kind of had an

Ellen DeGeneres look to her, with the exception of the tattoos and piercings. All of the wait staff wore white buttoned down shirts, black bottoms and shoes. Her uniform fit her nicely and you could tell she had a cute frame, any guy would love to have her on his arm, but it was clear that she played for the other team. And if I didn't think so by looking at her, she made it very clear by making a low grunting sound or moan, when I walked passed her. I turned to face her, to let her know that I heard her.

She smiled slightly and asked, "What is that fragrance you're wearing, it smells great?" I let her have her moment.

I simply replied, "Heat."

Once we made it to our tables she took our drink orders, I had water with lemon. No way was I going to have alcohol, the thought of it gave me a hangover. Kevin order a double shot of Hennessey. I knew he was nervous. I sat directly across from him, and watched his every move. I saw him staring at me, so I leaned forward a little further with my chest poked out as I pretended to read the menu. His eyes were deadlocked on my breasts. He couldn't help it; he always loved my breasts. I did notice that he wore the suit that I liked and he smelled amazing; however, the events that led up to our current situation left me with a bad taste in my mouth towards him. Right now, I found Kevin extremely unattractive. I waited a while before I interrupted his thoughts.

"Hey, you ok over there?" I asked.

"Huh? Oh, um, yeah. I'm good. Uh, you look nice. You got your hair done?" he asked.

"Thank you. Yeah, I got a touch-up this morning," I said, reaching up to touch my hair.

Again, his eyes were on my breasts as I interrupted his thoughts.

"Look, I'm gonna run to the restroom. If she comes back before I get back, order me the baked chicken with steamed broccoli, no butter," I said as I stood.

I moved slowly so he could take it all in. I was rocking a navy blue wrap dress that tied in the back. It hugged my midsection tight, forcing my Double-Ds to sit up perfectly. It hung loose around my hips, showing off the curve of my ass, allowing it to move swiftly as I walked. Thanks to the six-inch stilettos on my feet, my ass sat up nicely for the whole restaurant to take notice. I turned on my heels and sauntered towards the ladies' room. I glanced in the mirror in front of me, and saw that Kevin's eyes were glued to my ass. My plan was working perfectly.

Once in the restroom I checked my hair, made sure I didn't need more gloss on my lips and double-checked my outfit in the mirror. Satisfied, I checked my phone for any messages from Bianca. I saw a text letting me know she and Josh had made it to Chicago safely. I texted her back to have fun, and headed back to my table. When I got to the table, I saw Kevin hurrying to put his phone away.

"Who was that, your little girlfriend?" I asked, full of attitude.

"Huh?"

"If you can huh, you can hear! You heard me."

"Baby that was nobody..." he started to lie, but before he could get it out I asked the one question that has been on my mind since I left our home Saturday night.

"Who is she Kevin?"

"She who?" He tried to play dumbfounded.

"The bitch you fucked in our bed! Don't play stupid," I said, a little louder than I wanted to, but I was upset. Plus, the restaurant was so packed and loud that we could barely hear each other.

He was silent at first, probably trying to come up with another lie. Then, he finally said, "She was nobody."

"Oh no, she was definitely somebody because you fucked her at least three times in our bed. So, I will ask you again. Who is she?" I stated angrily.

I could feel my temperature rising with every breath I took. The more he stalled, looked away, and tried to calm me down, the angrier I became.

"Baby..." He began.

"Stop. Don't fucking call me that," I stated emphatically.

"I'm sorry. Bri, I love you, only you. I fucked up, and I'm sorry. Please let's work to get past this. I will do whatever you ask; we can go to counseling, whatever. Bay...I mean, Brianna, I just want you to come home," he pleaded.

None of that mattered to me. I needed to know who she was. Who was the woman that played a role in turning my life upside down? I wanted to know how she looked, what she had that I didn't, how long it lasted, how they met. I wanted answers that he clearly was not ready to give up. I stood up, ready to walk away. I gathered my things, and just as I turned to head for the door, he stood and grabbed my arm.

"Let me go, what the hell is your problem?" I yelled, drawing attention to our table.

"Look, sit down, so we can finish talking," he insisted.

"Kevin, you need to let me go."

Just then, the waitress walked up with our food in hand. She asked, "Is there a problem?"

"No, you can place the food down, and give us a minute please," Kevin responded still holding on to my arm.

The waitress gave me a look to see if I was ok, I gave her an assuring nod. She placed the food down, and walked away. I looked over at Kevin, and in the iciest tone that I could muster up, I said, "If you don't take your hands off of me…"

Before I could finish, he jerked me towards him and said, "Or what? Last time it was a lucky shot, but please believe it won't happen again."

I was about to go off on his ass, when I heard a male's voice behind me say, "Ay man. Look, I don't want no trouble, but the lady asked you to let her go."

I turned around to see the chocolate Adonis towering over Kevin and me, his two friends were behind him. Kevin, never being one to back down from a fight, mean mugged the guy and told him to mind his own business. The Adonis stood firm. He asked Kevin again, to release my arm and suggested that he go outside to cool off.

"Look man, it's crowded in here, all these folks around, you really don't need to have these folks in your business," the Adonis said.

Kevin thought about what he said and looked around the restaurant. All eyes were on us. I was so embarrassed. Kevin released my arm and I immediately did a beeline for the door, thinking I could never show my face in there again. I made it to my car, and noticed that the chocolate Adonis was right on my heels.

Kevin

"What the fuck are y'all looking at?!" I
yelled my frustrations at the people in the
restaurant, because I couldn't release it on Brianna.
The nerve of this Captain Save A Hoe ass clown to
come over and get in my business. I would've
fucked him up, but he did have a point, all these
white folks around and I definitely didn't want them
in my business. Hell, they probably called the
police already. I needed to get my shit and get the
fuck up out of there. I paid for the meals we didn't
eat, slammed the rest of my cognac and stormed out
of the restaurant.

Once outside I looked around for Brianna,
and saw her walking away with old boy. I couldn't
believe what I was seeing; it was like some shit out
of a Tyler Perry movie. Good guy comes along and
takes girl from bad, cheating, boyfriend. Get the
fuck outta here with that! I started to follow them,
but I looked down and saw shorty calling me, again.

"What the fuck you want!" I yelled.

"Baby, please don't do this," she started
pleading, and I hung up the phone.

I needed to get my head straight. I let Bri
and dude go for now, but she had better believe that
I'm coming for her ass real soon. I'm not just
gonna let her up and leave me, nah, not that easy.
I'm gonna get her back. First, I needed to handle
this little problem with shorty; she was getting way
outta line. I headed to my car so I could get away
from here before I did something stupid. Plus like I
said, the cops were probably on the way to arrest

my black ass. I needed to go home and get some rest. Today has been a fucked up day.

Brianna

"Gorgeous, Gorgeous, slow down. Are you ok?" he asked before I could get in my truck.

"What do you think?" I asked.

"Look, I don't know what that was about back there, but I do know you're in no condition to drive. Why don't you take a walk with me and cool off?" the Adonis offered.

He was right. I was shaking uncontrollably and the tears in my eyes blurred my vision. However, I was too stubborn to take him on his offer right away, even if he did help me out. I was just too embarrassed. He sensed my hesitation.

"Come on Gorgeous, I promise that I won't hurt you. I just want to make sure you're ok."

"Why do you care?"

"That's a good question. To be honest I don't know; maybe because I hate to see women cry."

His friends came out of the restaurant to check on him. I assumed that he was their ride, because he tossed one of them a set of keys and told them to go on without him.

"So, you're just gonna leave your friends like that? Don't let me bust up the party," I said.

"Nah, they're cool, I'd rather see about you anyway. So, what about that walk?"

Just then, Kevin came walking out of the restaurant. We locked eyes for a minute until he saw the tall chocolate brother standing next to me. He looked at me, and then back at the Adonis. This was just another chance for me to hit Kevin where it hurts.

"Ok, why not." I gave in to the Adonis' request.

As we walked off, I looked back at Kevin; he had a look of shock and resentment on his face. The look almost made me smile. I gave him a slight grin, and turned around to focus on what was ahead of me. I assume Kevin probably stood there for a moment still in shock, and then eventually walked to his car. I didn't turn back around to find out.

***

At first, we walked in an awkward silence. I didn't' know what to say, and I guess he didn't either, as we walked down the busy sidewalk, passing bars and lounges along the strip. I replayed the incident in the restaurant with Kevin in my head. What the hell got into him? He's never grabbed me before, never once threatened me. The man I saw tonight is a complete stranger to me. He was not the man I was going to marry. My thoughts were interrupted by the Adonis.

"So, what's your name Gorgeous?" he asked.

"Brianna, what's yours?"

"Brianna, that's a beautiful name for a beautiful woman," he said. "My name is Harley, but my friends call me Ryder, that's my last name."

I laughed. "Harley Ryder? For real?"

He smiled a bit embarrassed. "Yeah, I don't know what my parents were thinking. I got picked on so much in school, so I just dropped my first name and made everyone call me Ryder."

"I'm sorry, I don't mean to laugh, but that is pretty interesting."

"It's cool. I'm used to it."

"So, Harley, are you always rescuing damsels in distress?" I asked trying to lighten the mood.

"Nah, usually I don't butt into other folks business, but you looked like you could use a hand, or two."

"I appreciate that. I was so embarrassed." Remembering what just happened almost brought a new set of tears to my eyes. I looked away to fight off my tears. When I looked across the way, I thought I saw my sister's BFF Kris. Not wanting her to see me like this, I quickly turned around and faced Harley. He must have sensed my discomfort because he stopped walking and turned to me.

"It's cool Gorgeous. If you wanna talk about it, I'm a good listener," he said sincerely.

"So, you're still gonna call me Gorgeous even though I told you my name is Brianna huh?" I asked, trying to make light of a tense situation. As I said, it's a Williams' thing.

He laughed. "Ok, *Brianna*. You wanna talk about it? What's going on between you and your man?"

"He's not my man."

"Ok, so who is he?" he asked, fishing.

"He's my ex fiancé," I stated. "Hey, can we sit down and talk? These shoes ain't made for walking," I asked.

We headed over to one of the lounges and grabbed a table. A waitress came over and gave us drink and food menus. Since neither of us ate at

Lola's, we ordered some appetizers and lemonades. We made small talk until the food came, and I started to feel comfortable with him. We talked about work. He told me he owned a construction company, I told him I was an Account Executive for a local company. We found out that we both loved neo soul music and hip-hop, real hip-hop. We also found that we were both in our early thirties, no kids, and loved running. Also, that we were both single. I enjoyed spending time with him, and he was a great distraction from what was going on with me, but the inevitable conversation rose again.

"So, what's the story with you and old boy? How did he become your ex fiancé?" he asked.

"Long story short, he cheated while I was away for work this past week."

Harley had a look of surprise on his face and confusion.

"He cheated? On you?" he asked surprised.

"Yeah, why you say it like that?" I asked.

"Because you're beautiful, any man who's crazy enough to step out on you is a fool."

I smiled. "Thank you. But it had to be something to make him stray; we were only engaged three months."

"Aye, don't look at it like that. That was just God's way of telling you that He has something better for you in the works. From what you tell me, you have everything going for you. You're smart, beautiful, and successful; he just didn't know your worth."

"Thanks, Harley. I appreciate that."

We talked a little more about Kevin's and my relationship and I wanted to steer the conversation in another direction. So I asked Harley, "So, enough about me. Why are you single?"

"I guess I just haven't found the right woman to settle down with," he responded.

Immediately I put my guard back up. That statement for me, translated to "I have too many women to choose from and I'm still trying to decide which one I want to give all of my time to." He was a very attractive man, I'm sure there was some woman in the midst waiting for him, but I didn't push. I had already made up my mind that I was done with men for a while. I wanted some time alone to get back to me, find myself again, and take my time to find out what I really wanted.

We chatted some more about different things such as current events, new movies that were out, and shared some laughs. Before I knew it, we had been sitting in the lounge almost three hours. It was a little after eleven o'clock and the lounge started to get crowded.

Harley leaned over and asked me if I was tired. I told him no, and he suggested that we leave and go someplace else. I took his hand and he led the way out of the lounge. We headed back to my truck and he directed me downtown to the Water Street area. We came up to a large loft building. I assumed it was his house, and was hesitant to get out of the car. I reached for the door handle, and he immediately stopped me.

"Stay there, I will get that for you."

He hopped out of the car and came around to open my door. I stepped out of the truck and we walked hand in hand up to the lofts.

I asked, "Is this your place?"

"One of them, just wait and see," he said.

We walked into the building and took the elevator to the 10th floor. When we stepped off, he guided me down the hall to a corner loft. I waited for him to unlock to the door, and when I stepped in, it wasn't what I expected. It was a large loft, turned art studio. There were hardwood floors throughout and had an open concept layout. Exposed beams adorned the ceiling and painted pipes were along the walls. Paintings of local attractions hang on the walls along with some abstract artwork, a few portraits, and some paintings of nature. They were all beautiful. One that caught my eye was of a beautiful young woman, with a smile that was sure to light up the darkest room. I assumed she was an old girlfriend or current lover.

I asked, "Who is that? She's beautiful."

He smiled and said, "Thank you, that's my mom."

"Seriously, she looks great!"

"Yeah, she was a great woman. She passed away two years ago."

"Oh, I'm sorry to hear that," I said

"Thanks. Go ahead and take a look around, while I set up," he said as he headed into one of the rooms.

I walked through the lightly furnished loft. There was a 42-inch flat screen TV resting on top of a glass entertainment stand, and he had a futon, and a small desk and computer. That was all of the furniture in the whole place. I walked towards the kitchen and noticed he had enough alcohol to fully stock a bar sitting on the counter. The loft had two bedrooms; each bedroom had a private bathroom. The guest bedroom's bath was also accessible from the living room; I went inside to freshen up. When I came out, Harley had set up two painting easels, two barstools, and an assortment of paints on the balcony.

"What's all of this?" I asked.

"This," he said as he motioned towards the setup, "is what I do when I need to clear my head, release stress, or get rid of pent up negative energy."

I was so surprised, all I could say was, "Oh.

"Come on." He grabbed my hand and led me to one of the stools and an easel that held a blank canvas. A little hesitant, I responded, "I've never painted before."

"Don't worry about that. Here, put this on. I don't want you to ruin that dress," he said with a smile, handing me an apron.

As I slid on the apron, Harley came up behind me to help me tie it up. I could've had done it myself, but I guess it was his way of being able to look at my ass up close and personal. He stayed behind me a little too long, making his intention extremely obvious. Once he secured the apron, he whispered in my ear, "Just relax." The smell of his sweet breathe filled my nostrils, along with the smell of his cologne. I was so caught up in my drama with Kevin that I didn't notice how good he smelled. I had to admit, the heat from his breathe in my ear sent tingles throughout my body.

I sat down on the stool. He rubbed my shoulders to lessen the tension. The feelings of his strong hands on my skin almost made me melt. Against my will, I let out a slight moan. That must have been his cue to go further. His hands trailed down my arms, squeezing lightly and rubbing out the tension. He massaged my hands, then his hands trailed back up to my shoulders, but not before he massaged my lower back and up my spine. This man sure was good with his hands. With every spot he touched I relaxed and slowly melted. So much so, that when he was done, I was sure that I needed a new pair of panties. I exhaled and opened my eyes. As I sat on the barstool, Harley behind me just finishing my massage, I slightly spread my legs apart to let the cool breeze up my dress and dry the river threatening to form between my thighs.

He stepped away and my body begged him to come back. I gathered my composure and softly said, "Thanks, I really needed that."

"No problem. Would you like a glass of wine?"

"Yes, white please."

Harley came back with two glasses of wine, and then we got started on our paintings. He told me to paint how I felt right now. It's amazing how one person can make all the difference. Before Harley came along, I was pissed off, hurt, and out to hurt Kevin in the worst way. But now, even though I am still hurt and wounded from what Kevin did to me, I feel relaxed. I feel at peace; I feel sexy and desired. I painted flowers in a meadow, using a lot of bright colors to reflect my mood. I painted butterflies, and a big yellow sun. I painted all things that reflected happiness and good energy. They were also the only things that I could paint or draw that would be recognizable to anyone other than me.

I was so caught up in my painting that I hadn't realized that my phone was buzzing. I reached in to my purse and looked to see who was calling. It was Kevin. I pressed ignore, turned off my phone, and got back to my painting. Once finished, I took a look at my painting and laughed.

"What's so funny?" Harley asked.

"My artwork is horrible. A five year old would have done better."

"I'm sure it's fine, let me take a look," Harley said as he got up from his barstool.

He came over and took a look at my painting, "Yeah, you're right. That's awful," he laughed.

"Thanks a lot, let me see what yours look like."

I walked over to his easel and stopped when I saw the image that he created. It was beautiful. It was a sketched image of me painting, in what looked like black chalk. He caught every detail; the smirk on my face as I imagined myself chasing butterflies through the meadow, the dimple in my right cheek, the way my hair was twisted up on top of my head. He even added the detail on my earrings. I was speechless.

"Do you like it?" he asked.

"I love it, this is incredible," I responded.

"Good. Keep it."

"Really? Thanks. You can have mine too. I know it's not as good as yours, but…"

"It's beautiful," he interrupted.

For a moment, we stood in silence trying to read each other. I broke the awkward silence, "It's getting late, and I should probably head home."

"Ok, I think I will stay here at the studio tonight and have my friend bring my car back in the morning," he said.

"I can take you home, or to your car if you'd like," I said.

"You sure you're not too tired?"

"I'm fine."

"Ok cool, let me call him and see where he's at."

Harley

I watched her as she walked over to the futon and took a seat, then proceeded to the kitchen to call my boy Jason about my car. All the while, I prepared for him to clown me about taking up for Brianna. I don't know what the hell I was thinking; it was just something about her smile that made me gravitate to her. From the moment we locked eyes coming into the restaurant, I knew I had to have her. Not to mention, it did kinda piss me off to see dude grabbing on her. I don't know, but something in me couldn't stay out of it. So, against my better judgment and the advice from my boys, here I am with this beautiful woman in my studio, not wanting our night to end. I caught myself starring at her again when my boy picked up the phone.

"Yo, Ryder what up man? I thought you might have ran off to Vegas with shorty or something," he said laughing.

"Nah man, it ain't even like that."

"So what's up, you need me to come scoop you?"

"No need. Where you at?"

"I'm at the crib now. Where you at?" he asked.

"Downtown, I will be there in twenty minutes, be looking out."

"Ok cool, peace." Jason hung up.

I cleaned up the patio and put everything away. After washing the paintbrushes and setting them aside to dry. I rolled up the picture of Brianna I drew, tied a ribbon around it, and gave it to her. She flashed that beautiful smile at me again, and it took everything in me not to grab her and lay her down on the futon. However, I remained a gentleman and asked, "Are you ready to go?" I held out my hand, she grabbed it and followed me out the door.

"You want me to drive?" I asked

"Why, you don't like the way I drive?" she asked jokingly.

"No, I didn't mean that at all. I just figured you might be tired that's all. Plus, a man is supposed to drive anyway."

She stopped walking and stood still for a minute. She crossed her arms over her chest and asked, "Oh really?" She laughed and continued walking. "That's nice, but I think I got this."

I laughed and raised my hands up and said, "Alright then, get it."

We laughed and talked a bit while waiting for the elevator to come. Once inside, even though it was empty, I backed up against the wall and pulled her in front of me. I felt a slight shiver escape from her as I wrapped my arms around her and whispered in her ear.

"You're beautiful, and I had a great time with you."

"Me too, thank you for turning my night around."

The elevator came to a stop, and for a second neither of us moved. We exited and headed to her truck. I helped her in, and walked around to the passenger side to get in. After telling her where to go, we eased out into traffic and headed to pick up my car. I sat back and thought about how I was going to make sure that she stuck around. I had a good feeling about her that I haven't had for any woman in a long time.

Brianna

Moments later we were on highway 45 headed south to pick up his car. It was out of my way, but I didn't mind. Part of me was not ready to end our night. On our way to his friend's house, we made small talk about our families. I told him about my sisters and learned he was his mother's only child. We swapped stories about our childhood all the way through our college life. Before we knew it, we were in front of his friend's house where he needed to pick up his car.

"Wait right here, I'm gonna run in and grab my keys. Then I will follow you home."

"You don't have to do that, I'm a big girl."

"I know, but it's late and I want to make sure you get home safe."

"Ok."

Harley ran inside to get his keys and after a few moments, he came out and hopped into an all-black SUV. I pulled forward to let him out of the driveway, and before I knew it, we were headed to my place. As I drove, I kept telling myself, "I will not fuck him, I will not fuck him." As bad as I wanted to, it would end up being a revenge fuck, and I didn't want that. I liked Harley and all, but his timing just couldn't be worst. I needed to deal with Kevin first. There was no way I was letting him get away with grabbing me like that. He must have lost his damn mind. But I'm not gonna trip, I'm gonna enjoy the rest of my night and figure out how to get back at Kevin tomorrow. And, I WILL find out who this mystery bitch is.

After saying good night to Harley and promising to call him, I popped open a bottle of wine and replayed the night's events. It didn't go as I planned; I mean, yes, Kevin saw me and wanted me, but I didn't get the information I sought. I had to know who this woman was. He wouldn't even tell me her name. He wouldn't tell me how they met or how long their affair have been going on; and I knew for a fact it wasn't the same chick he cheated on me with before, she was long gone. After a few hours, I gave up and retreated to my bedroom, feeling dizzy and regretting not inviting Harley in.

Chapter Four

Brianna

The next day, I got out of bed a little before noon. It was a nice day out, so I decided to go for a run. I threw on a pair of shorts, tennis shoes, and a tank top and headed to the park. I always drove to the park to do my runs, I didn't care for running along the city sidewalks, and there were too many distractions and too many streetlights interrupting my flow. The park was the perfect place for me to run. They had an awesome three-mile trail that included a killer hill, but the best part was the small waterfall. I love to stop there after my workout and just watch the running water, listening to the water crashing on the rocks; it helped me clear my head.

When I pulled into the park, I saw Kris standing in the parking lot stretching; no surprise, we all ran here, sometimes together. She looked stressed; I walked over to say hi.

"Hey lady! You coming or going?" I asked.

"Hey girl," Kris said. She looked a little surprised to see me. She asked, "How you been"?

We hugged a bit. I could swear I smelled Kevin, but it could be my mind playing tricks on me. He's been invading all of my senses since this shit popped off.

"I'm living. I know Brooke told you everything that's been going on," I said.

"Yeah, that's messed up. So, what you gonna do?" she asked, still stretching.

"Haven't figured that out yet, but after last night, I'm definitely through with his ass. I will tell you about it later."

"Ok, cool."

"Hey, you want some company? I'm doing the whole three miles," I asked.

"Sure, me too," she said.

We ran in silence, both of us listening to our iPods. It was nice running with Kris; I've always been fond of her. She and Brooke have been best friends since junior high. She doesn't have any siblings, she grew up in a foster home, and we've become her family. Bianca and I have always treated her like an older sister. With my other two sisters enjoying their weekend getaways, I was happy to spend some time with Kris. After our run, we went to grab salads from a local sandwich shop and made plans to meet at the house for dinner and a movie.

***

When I got home, I noticed a huge bouquet of flowers on the porch. Probably from one of Bianca's flavor of the months, but the arrangement was beautiful. I got out of my truck to grab the flowers and take them inside. There was a note attached, and the envelope had my name on it. Immediately, I wanted to throw the flowers out, I knew they were from Kevin. I unlocked the front door ready to rush inside and throw the flowers in the trash. I walked to the kitchen and set everything down on the table. I opened the small envelope to read the card inside,

Have a great day Gorgeous. Always, Ryder

I smiled after reading the card, and decided that I liked Harley and wanted to keep him around. I called him to thank him for the flowers. The phone rang a few times before he picked up, "Hey Gorgeous," he answered. The sexiness in his voice oozing through the phone made my panties wet. I was already sweaty from the run and needed to shower, badly.

"Um hey, Harley, how are you?" I asked.

He laughed a bit, "I'm good. How are you Gorgeous?"

"I'm great, what's so funny?" I asked, thrown off course.

"Nothing major, just that you're the only one in the world who calls me Harley, that's all.

"Oh, well, that's your name," I responded. "Plus, you're the only one who calls me *Gorgeous*."

"Ok, Ok, my bad, *Brianna,*" he said laughing.

I smiled and laughed a bit, and got back to the reason I called. "Anyway, I called to tell you thank you for the flowers. They are *beautiful*."

"No problem Gorgeous. I saw them and thought of you. I just wanted to thank you for a great night last night. I enjoyed spending time with you."

"Me too."

"So, you got any plans tonight?" he asked.

"Actually I do. My sister and I are going to cook and watch some movies tonight."

"Oh, ok, ok. Maybe me and my guy can stop by and join you. Is that cool?"

"Sure, she's single and as long as he ain't butt ugly I'm sure she won't mind," I said.

"What time you thinking?" he asked.

"Let's do seven, that'll give us time to cook and have the food ready."

"Sounds good, I'll talk to you later Gorgeous," he said, and hung up.

After getting off the phone with Harley, I wondered what just happened. I mean, I appreciated the flowers and all, but I didn't think I was ready to have him meet my sister and meet his friends. However, I quickly got over it. I had a great time with Harley, he was good company, plus I was curious to see what Kris thought of him. I valued her opinion just as much as I valued Brooke and Bianca's opinion on decisions I made. I became surprisingly excited about tonight, and hurried to the shower so I could start getting things together.

***

It was around 5 o'clock when Kris showed up with a few bags of groceries and some movies neither of us made the time to go see at the theater. When I opened the door for her, I was in the middle of a heated argument with Kevin. He had the audacity to call me, questioning me about leaving the restaurant with Harley. I opened the front door, took one of the bags from Kris and guided her to the kitchen with Kevin screaming in my ear as if he lost his damn mind.

"Kevin, I don't have time for this. We can talk about who I left with when you tell me who you're fucking," I said, and disconnected the call.

"You aight sis?" Kris asked, sounding concerned.

"Yeah, I'm good," I said. And before I could ask her what movies that she brought, she yelled out, "No that sonofabitch didn't send you flowers!"

"What? No, those are from Harley," I said laughing. Kris was just like Brooke when it came to being over protective.

"Oh, I was gonna say. You don't fuck somebody and then send flowers to apologize," she seethed.

"Right, or call me questioning me about who I'm with and my business. I stopped being his business when he fucked that bitch in our house," I said. I felt myself getting angry and needed to calm down, so I started taking the items in the grocery bags out, and placing them on the counter.

"True. But wait a minute, who is Harley? I am so out of the loop, Brooke didn't mention you were seeing someone," Kris said.

"Oh, I'm not. I met him the other day at the restaurant when I met up with Kevin. Kevin started tripping and grabbed me. He wouldn't let me leave, so Harley came over and helped me out."

"He grabbed you? Kevin? I've never known Kevin to get physical with anyone."

"Me either. Imagine my surprise. I was so embarrassed, but Harley made me feel better. We hung out that night so I could cool off. Oh, and he's coming by with a friend of his tonight." I tried to say that last part fast enough that she wouldn't notice, but she picked right up on it.

"Whoa, hold up. You didn't tell me this was turning into a double date," she said.

"I know, but it just sorta happened. I thought you might want to meet somebody new," I replied.

"Damn, Bri you shoulda told me. I'm actually I kinda seeing somebody." "Kinda, means it's not official. And since when?"

"Since, I started seeing them. Besides, I look a mess."

"You're fine, but if you wanna change, go upstairs and find something. We wear the same size," I offered.

"You owe me heffa." She said and left the kitchen.

While she got dressed, I started dinner. We had baked chicken, mac and cheese, cabbage, and cornbread. For dessert, we had ice cream and all the toppings to make sundaes. After Kris changed into a pink sweat suit, similar to the purple one I was wearing, we set the table and prepared for our guests. While waiting, I gave her the details on Harley and our night out. She seemed genuinely interested, but I could tell she was a little distracted. I asked her if she was ok, and she said she was fine. I figured she was just nervous about meeting Harley's friend.

The guys showed up just in time, because I had just taken the mac and cheese out the oven. Kris answered the door and I could hear everyone greeting each other.

"Hey come on in. I'm Kris, Brianna's sister, and you are?"

"How are you doing? I'm Ryder and..." Harley started, and Kris, interrupted him and turned towards his friend.

"And you must be Harley?" she asked.

"No, my name is Jason, he's Harley," Jason responded.

Harley laughed and said, "My name is Harley, but my friends call me Ryder."

"Oh, Harley Ryder, that's interesting. Well come on in, Bri is in the kitchen. We just finished cooking."

She led the guys into the kitchen and as they walked in, Harley stated, "Damn, it smell good in here. Y'all must've did y'all thang!"

"Well you know, this is what we do," I said smiling.

Harley came over to me and embraced me with the biggest hug. I loved the way I felt in his arms.

"How are you doing Gorgeous? You look great," he said as he released me.

"Thank you, so do you," I said.

"So, shall we eat?" Kris interrupted.

"Good idea Kris. Why don't you show them where the bathroom is so they can wash their hands? I will set everything out," I said.

Kris led them to the first floor bathroom and I walked over to the stove to grab the food. I stopped when I heard a phone vibrating. I looked around on the kitchen counter to see of it was mine, but I found Kris's phone ringing. I started to grab it and give it to her, but the number on the screen stopped me in my tracks. It was Kevin calling.

Kris

I have to admit, Jason was kinda cute, but Harley, was fine! I mean, the brother had it going on, and those dreads... Yeah, Bri did good. She did real good. I knew Jason liked what he saw when he looked at me and if this was about six months ago, I would have been all for it. But like I said, I had somebody. I just had to figure out a way to tell my sisters. It was going to be hard, they might even get upset about it, but eventually it had to be done. Right now, I'm not gonna worry about it though. I will just enjoy the company of these two fine men. I lead the gentlemen to the restroom and retreated back to the kitchen, to help Bri set the table.

"Girl, he is fine!" I said, trying to sound excited. At least I wasn't lying.

"Who? Oh um, Jason. Yeah he's cute," she responded. I sensed something was wrong so I asked, "What's up Bri? You ok?"

"Yeah, just that Kevin is working my damn nerves. You know, he just called you. He is so low! Since I won't answer my phone, he's calling my sisters now?" She was fuming. I thought to myself, *damn, why I didn't take my phone with me.*

"Don't trip, Bri. He's called a few times, but I haven't spoken to him. Don't let him get under your skin. Y'all broke up, so we broke up with him too. Now, smile and enjoy your date, with his fine ass." I laughed trying to lighten the mood.

"Yeah you right. Thanks sis, I love you." She smiled.

I smiled back, but I felt like shit. Here I was lying to one of the most important people in my life.

She and her sisters were all the family I had, and I couldn't trust them enough not to disown me if I told them how my life has changed these last six months and what I've been up to. Worst part is, Kevin's the only other person who knows and he's adamant about me not telling Bri and the girls right now. Not to mention, the fact that Kevin was so reckless to leave condom wrappers all over the floor and now he's on the Williams sisters' hit list. It's only a matter of time before they found out that I've been lying to them this whole time. Kevin can't be trusted. I know he would throw me under the bus just to take the heat off himself. I was in such a messed up position.

Brianna wore so much heartache on her face. It was invisible to the blind eye, but I could see it. She really loves Kevin and she's trying to move on, but I can tell she's confused. She doesn't know whether she wants to kill him or go back to him. I can't blame her; I've been there myself. There's no way I could tell her now, she has too much on her plate and this would only make matters worse and more confusing. I had to wait for the right time, until then, my lips were sealed.

After setting the table and everyone sat down to eat, I was able to relax a bit and enjoy the conversation.

"So Kris, you've never seen *The Lion King*? That's crazy! What kind of childhood did you have growing up, that deprived you of such a classic movie?" Jason laughed.

Jason and Ryder started laughing. Bri and I just looked at each other with an awkward stare.

"Actually, I bounced around from foster home to foster home. Never really settled anyplace long enough to watch a movie." I grinned to relieve the tension.

"Oh damn, I'm sorry to hear that ma. My bad," Jason said apologetically.

"Well, now that everybody's plates are clean, how about you two go ahead and get the movie setup, while we put the food away real quick," Brianna directed to Jason and me.

"Ok cool. Lead the way Beautiful," Jason said to me.

We walked to the front room in silence. I fumbled with the DVD player for a while and popped the movie in. I was so nervous around him, but I didn't know why. Maybe it was the brief flashback, I had to my childhood; that always unsettled me. I quickly regained my composure and sat down on the other end of the couch that Jason sat on.

"You can move a little closer, I don't bite," he said and smiled. He had an incredible smile, I didn't notice before.

I moved closer and left enough room for Bri and Ryder to sit with us. They were taking way too long in the kitchen. I wanted to get up and go get them, but Jason stopped me before I could get up.

"Hey, I hope you're not upset about the stupid comment I made earlier. I didn't mean anything by it. Believe me, had I known I wouldn't have been so insensitive…" he started rambling, so I cut him off.

"It's cool. The past is the past, and I'm good now," I said.

We locked eyes for a minute, until we were interrupted by my phone buzzing. I looked down to see Kevin calling.

"I better take this," I said.

I got up and walked to the bathroom for a little privacy.

"Hello," I answered.

"What's up, why you ain't answering your phone?" he asked.

"I'm at the house with Brianna, we ate and are about to watch some movies. And she saw you calling me!" I said.

"Oh shit! What did she say?" he asked.

"She was pissed. She thinks you're harassing us since she won't talk to you."

"What else she say?"

"Nothing really. We have company right now, so she's a bit distracted."

"We? Company? Who?"

"She invited her friend by and he brought his guy. What's the big deal? You're mad? Want your cake and eat it too, huh? "I asked a bit annoyed.

"The dread head dude?" he asked, but before I responded yelled, "Aw hell nah! I'm on my way." Then, the call disconnected.

"Hello?" I said. I looked at the screen, and it was back to the home screen picture. I had to go warn Brianna that Kevin was on his way.

I practically ran out of the bathroom, and bumped right into Jason.

"You ok ma? I was just coming to check on you," he said.

"Uh, yeah I'm good, where's Bri?" I asked.

"They're on the couch. We're about to start the movie..." he said, but I was already headed that way.

"Bri, can I talk to you for a second?" I asked.

"Yeah what's up?" she said and headed to where I was standing. I led her back towards the bathroom and told her what was up.

"Kevin just called, and I didn't want to be rude in front of Jason so I answered the phone. I basically told him to go away, stop calling and that he was ruining our evening. However, he said he was on his way and hung up," I lied. I watched her as her face changed from confusion, to horror, to anger.

"What! He got some nerve! He better not show up here, if he knows what's good for him," she said.

"What do you think we should do? Maybe we should tell Jason and Ryder they gotta bounce," I suggested.

"Hell no! Harley ain't going no place. I'm not letting Kevin ruin our night. Come on," she said and grabbed my arm leading us to the front room.

I didn't like how this was going, and I had a feeling this wasn't gonna turn out well for somebody. I just didn't know who, and I prayed that somebody wasn't me.

Kevin

After hanging up the phone with Kris, I was livid. I couldn't believe Brianna was still kicking it with this clown. It's bad enough she left the damn restaurant with him, leaving me there to look like a damn fool. She can't be serious the brother ain't even all that! And don't get me started on Kris; she was being real foul right now and she knew it. I needed to get over there and set some shit straight! I didn't know dude or his homeboy he had with him, so I definitely wasn't going over there naked.

I walked over to the closet and grabbed my gun out the safe. I checked the clip to make sure it was still fully loaded and placed the gun behind my back in the waist of my pants. I grabbed my jacket and car keys to head over to Bri's house. By the time I made it to my car, I was already having second thoughts. "What the hell am I doing?" I asked myself aloud. I sat in silence thinking about all the bullshit that led me to this point. If only I could've just stuck with my original plan to keep things platonic between shorty and me, I wouldn't be sitting here contemplating taking that fool out and risking my freedom.

I needed to clear my head before I did something stupid and since I couldn't call Bri, for obvious reasons, I called my attorney and longtime friend Dee.

"I was wondering when you would call me back," she said when she answered.

"Look, chill. I'm stressing enough as it is," I said.

"What's going on?" she asked.

97

"Brianna," I responded.

"What about her?" she asked as if she wasn't interested in hearing what I had to say.

"She got some clown at her crib right now." I couldn't even believe the words that were coming out of my mouth.

"So?" she asked confused.

"So! What the hell do you mean so? That's my woman!" I yelled at the phone.

"The woman you cheated on, if I remember correctly. You fucked up, not her. Let it go Kev!" she said.

"Oh, so it's like that?" I asked.

"Look, that's y'all business. We wouldn't even be having this conversation if you…"

"If I what?" I cut her off. "What? Fucked with you? You didn't know what you wanted until I proposed to her!" She was really pissing me off.

"Aight fine, so what? You gonna go over there and do what besides get yourself locked up over a bitch who don't want you?" she asked.

"First, don't ever, ever, call my girl a bitch if you know what's good for you and you wanna keep your job."

"Yeah ok, heard that before," she said.

"Aight smart ass. You get those contracts renewed for my DJs?" I asked, wanting to change the conversation.

"Yes, I did. I will meet you at the club later to have you sign them. You ready for the after party?" she asked sounding excited. Just that quick I forgot about the major concert that was going on this weekend with the after party being at my club,

Silhouette. There was big money to be made tomorrow night. Big money; that always put a smile on my face, and I could hear the smug ass smile on Dee's face cause she knew she had just changed my mood.

"Damn, how did I let that slip my mind? Hell yeah I'm ready. You get all the contracts finalized for the guest appearances?" I asked.

"Of course I did," she responded.

"Cool, I'm about to head to the club now and check on my liquor delivery," I said.

"Oh, so you're not going over to Bri's and busting up the party?" She laughed.

"Nah, you can though," I said intentionally to pique her interest.

"What? Why do I need to go over there?" she asked.

"Nothing man, see you later" I said hanging up.

I knew she would sweat me about it later, but that's what her ass get for talking shit. I'm glad I called her though, because I definitely needed to get my head right for tomorrow night. Every year around this time, Milwaukee had a huge concert to promote the initiative to stop gun violence in the city. The lineup this year was crazy, and Dee worked some of her connects to get a few of the performers to do appearances at my club for the after party.

Having celebrities at the club was nothing new, but I always had to be on top of my game. Milwaukee is a small city and the competition for the nightlife was real. Not only were clubs competing against each other for the crowds, but we were also competing with the local politicians who wanted to see us shut down. I had it the worst of them all being one of the few Black club owners in the city, and the youngest. I had to stay on top of my game; I had no choice. Therefore, I needed to put the bullshit that I had going on with Brianna on pause, and focus on this money.

I started up my car and headed to the club, making sure to ride passed Brianna's house even though it was out of the way. I saw Bri's X6 parked in the driveway in front of the garage, with Kris's Maxima parked next to it. Directly in front of the house was an all-black Benz truck. I slowed down a bit to try to look through the bay windows, but I couldn't see much from the street. Just when I was about to pull off, the curtain moved and I saw Kris standing in the window and she looked straight at me. I nodded and continued on to the club.

Kris

I almost shit a brick when I saw Kevin lurking outside. I knew for sure shit was about to hit the fan. I began to panic, we locked eyes for a second and then he just drove off. I expected him to circle back around, so I waited before I left the window to go back and watch the movie. As I stood there, I thought back to a time when I was most happy. When I first met the love of my life, everything was perfect then. It was during the grand opening of Kevin's club Silhouette's new location. The old building was too small for the crowds he was attracting, so he moved to a bigger building in downtown Milwaukee. He now owned the largest nightclub in the city.

Months prior to the grand opening, myself, Bri, Bianca, Brooke and Matt, all pitched in to help Kevin get things in order. We spent a lot of late nights getting that place together, and it was there, that I met my love. I stood there and reminisced about the night the club opened in the new location.
***

I had fallen asleep on the couch and was awakened by something vibrating against my cheek. At first, I thought I was tripping until I opened my eyes and noticed I was laying partially on my cell phone. I looked down at my phone screen. I smiled when I saw a picture of my baby smiling back at me.

"Hey baby," I answered.

I heard the sounds of traffic and heavy wind in the background before hearing,

"I'm outside, buzz me in."

I hung up the phone and peeled myself off the couch. Tightening my black satin robe, I walked across the room to the door. On my way, I peaked at the time on my DVR box, 9:17 PM. I thought to myself, I don't have much time to get ready. I hit the button on the intercom to unlock the main door; I unlocked the door to my apartment, and retreated to my bedroom.

I opened the doors to my walk in closet to glance at my extensive wardrobe. Racks of designer clothes hung in the balance, a lot of them still with price tags on them. I thought to myself, what am I going to wear tonight? I reached for the newest addition to my collection, a royal blue mini dress that I tried on earlier that week and had to have. It fit my 5 foot 5 inch, 145-pound frame just right. I turned to the mirror and held the dress up against my robe. This will be perfect. As I admired how the dress complimented my dark skin, I felt a set of cold hands wrap around my eyes.

"Guess who?"

I laughed and turned around to a welcoming deep kiss. Cold soft lips, turned warm by a combination of body heat and hot tongues.

I stepped back to break the embrace, but not before giving my baby one last peck.

"It's good to see you too," I said with a smile.

My baby looked at me as if caught in a trance. I loved that look. Every time, it gave me a tingle down my spine that went directly to my sweet spot. I always knew what to expect after that. I thought to myself, do I have time? After battling my hormones, I shook my head.

"Uh-uh, not now. We don't have time to fool around. I'm already late," I said.

However, my baby's mind was already made up.

"It won't take long for what I want to do."

Before I knew it, our lips were locked again, and I was being led away from my closet. I dropped my dress, and fell onto my bed.

Breaking our embrace once again, I looked into those beautiful brown eyes and submitted.

"Ok, let's make this quick so we can go," I said.

I untied my robe to reveal my naked body. I saw my baby hesitate then take in the sight, but she; YES SHE; did not take off her dress. Instead, she slipped off her stiletto heels and fell down to her knees. Before I could speak, I felt her place soft kisses above my belly ring. She then, trailed her tongue down until she gripped my ring between her teeth. She tugged a little, and dipped her tongue into my belly button. I could feel the heat from her tongue and it made my clit throb with anticipation.

As she continued her slow seduction south, my anticipation grew with every kiss, and intensified with every stroke of her tongue. She wrapped her hands around my hips and brought me closer to her, her tongue never leaving my skin. My ass hung partially off the edge of the bed. I gripped the sheets to subdue the urge I had to grab her head and force her to my awaiting clitoris. She spread my legs wider and trailed kisses up my thighs, then with her tongue followed the same trail all the way up to my sex. I could no longer resist. I thrusted my hips forward and started to squirm in response to her tease. She grabbed my waist and without hesitation dove in.

Sucking and pulling on my clit in a way that only she could drove me crazy! Two manicured thumbs spread my lips wide and gave her full access to my hotspot. She released me from her mouth and placed a soft kiss on my clit. My abdominal muscles tightened and my sex muscles twitched in response. She spread my lips further apart, darted out her tongue and it stroked my clit. First slow, steady strokes then she gradually picked up the pace. With each contact, I felt the heat rising inside of me. My breath quickened, and I let out a low moan. Oh, shit this feels so good. My sex muscles contracted, I threw my head back further into my mattress and gripped the sheets tighter.

"Oh baby! I'm about to come," I screamed out.

She picked up the pace, and as I let my climax take over me, she slowed the strokes on my clit and sucked it gently. Soft moans escaped her as she licked and sucked up my release as if it's melted ice cream, while I lay paralyzed by ecstasy.

She placed one last kiss on my lower lips before standing to retrieve her shoes. I was left lying in a daze with a "just fucked" look on my face. I longed to return the favor, but I just didn't have the time. I rolled over onto my side and looked at my baby. She was bent over buckling the strap on her stilettos.

I remember thinking; damn she's fine. Long dark legs and thick calves spilled from the fire red mini dress. As I continued to watch her, my eyes traveled up her legs and I could see she was not wearing any panties. I continued my gaze up to her ass, nice, round and firm. It was almost better than mine, almost. As she stood and turned around, I continued my journey up her small waist, to her 36D breast. Yes, my baby was a beast!

That night, she rocked a fresh Brazilian Blowout, which let her hair cascade over her shoulders. I watched her reapply her lip-gloss on her thick soft lips. Her eyebrows were perfectly arched, and she was smiling through those big beautiful brown eyes. Yeah, she was ready.

I glanced over at the clock on my nightstand behind me; it was after 9:30 PM. I had to get ready. I sat up on the bed, but couldn't hide the grin that spread across my face. Deanna sat down on the bed next to me while I reached over and kissed her. When I dipped my tongue in her mouth, I could taste my release and it turned me on. It was just something about tasting me on her lips that made me so aroused. I started a soft sucking on her tongue as I kissed her. Her hands found their way to my breast and she pinched my nipples between her thumb and forefinger. I released her tongue and let out a low moan,

"Aaah."

She kissed my neck and whispered in my ear, "Time to get ready."

Then she kissed my cheek, and stood up.

"I'll go make you a drink, get ready so we can go."
***

That was Dee; she always got what she wanted, when she wanted it. She always had to be in charge, which was one of the things I loved about her. I was tired of hiding my sexuality from my sisters. It was time that I let them know about Dee and me. If they didn't accept me, so be it. I was happy with her and I planned to stay with her no matter what anyone else thought. I just had to find the right way to let it all out before Kevin said something. Ever since he caught us in Dee's office at the club, he's been tripping on me. You would think I was his woman or something. I knew it was a matter of time before he outed me, and I wasn't gonna give him the satisfaction.

As I stood there with my thoughts, Bri walked up.

"Girl, get away from this window. Kevin may be crazy, but he ain't stupid. He knows not to come over here, ain't no sense in worrying about that fool."

"Yeah you're right. I just don't want no drama," I said.

"Me either and it ain't none. Now, let's finish this movie," she said and directed me back to the couch.

We finished watching the movies and sat around to talk for a while. It started getting late, so I made an excuse to leave. I wanted to check in on Dee before I went home for the night. Jason and Ryder were leaving at the same time, so Jason offered to walk me to my car. We chatted outside for a while, I explained to him I was in a relationship and he accepted it. I got in my car and drove off, heading towards the club.

Chapter Five

Brooke

I paced back and forth across the bedroom floor as I listened to Bianca's ring back tone. "Come on B, damn! Pick up the phone," I said aloud. Matt was sound asleep in the bed. I knew he would flip out if he knew what I was about to do, but he didn't understand the bond that my sisters and I shared. He was an only child; he didn't have many close family members around. He had a few friends, but nothing is like family. He always hated for me to get into my sisters' troubles, but their troubles were mine, period.

"Hello?" Bianca answered.

"B, you're not gone believe what Kris just told me!" I said.

"What?" she asked "And it better be good since you calling me this damn late, interrupting my shit."

"Kevin fuckin Dee!" I practically screamed. I looked over and saw Matt turning over. When it looked like he was back to sleep, I stepped out the room.

"What! Dee from the club? The lawyer bitch?" she asked.

"Yup, and I know, I thought she was gay too," I said, already knowing what she was going to say.

"Damn! That's fucked up! What did Bri say?" she asked.

"She don't know yet. Kris just called and told me she caught them in Dee's office fucking on the floor behind the desk," I said.

"So, what did she do?" Bianca asked. I started laughing. I couldn't wait to tell her this part.

"She said she just blacked out and kicked her ass. She said that Kevin had to get security to help him get her off Dee. But he had to get dressed first, so by the time security got there, she had already gotten the best of her," I said, still laughing.

"Damn! I gotta get there, don't tell Bri until I get there. She gone snap! Where Kris at now?" she asked.

"She said she was on her way home. It sounded like she was crying. She was pretty upset. I know this whole situation has been a lot on all of us," I said. "I will call her in the morning."

"Ok, I will be back first thing tomorrow," said Bianca.

"Ok see you later," I said and hung up the phone.

When I went back in the room, Matt was wide-awake. He was sitting up on the bed and I know he heard our whole conversation by the look on his face. I tried to avoid him and climb in the bed, but he grabbed me by my gown and pulled me to the floor next to him.

"You just don't listen do you?" he seethed.

"Baby, you don't understand, that's my baby sister…" I couldn't continue because he grabbed my neck.

"Get out, and sleep on the couch. Not the guest room; on the fucking couch. You hear me?" he yelled.

I moved my head up and down as much as I could because I couldn't speak. He released my neck and threw a pillow down at me. Then, as if nothing happened, he climbed under the sheets and closed his eyes to go back to sleep. I hurried off the floor, grabbed the pillow and ran out the room. I went downstairs to the living room, climbed on the couch and started crying. These last few months have been hell, and I needed to get out of it. I didn't know how I was gonna do it, but I was no longer going to be Matt's punching bag. I pulled the throw over me and tried to get some sleep. First thing tomorrow, I was going to check on my sister.
***

The next morning, I woke up to Matthew standing over me. I was startled and jumped up knocking over the vase of lilies he bought me.

"I'm so sorry, baby, you scared me. I will clean it up right now," I said, scared shitless that he would go off on me. I started to get up.

"It's ok baby, relax. About last night, I'm sorry I let my anger get the best of me. I bought you these flowers; I know they're your favorite. And I got you this," he said, as he held up a new diamond tennis bracelet.

Under any other circumstances, I would have been thrilled and jumping for joy, but I've seen this same routine two other times before, and now I just felt sick to my stomach. He really thought that he could buy his way out of how he was treating me! For the past four months, I've been living in fear in my own house and he thought he could take it all away with flowers and a damn tennis bracelet. I was insulted, but I was no fool. I played nice to avoid him physically hurting me again. I began to cry, I was scared and the man that I love was the reason why. I was hurt, and angry.

"Thank you baby, it's beautiful," I said through tears.

Matthew grabbed me and hugged me tight. "Baby, don't cry. I'm so sorry B. I don't know why I've been tripping lately. I've just been so stressed out with work and everything. That's no excuse; I promise I will change. I will get help; do whatever it takes. I love you."

"I love you too Mathew," I said, and I meant it, but I knew in my heart that I couldn't stay. I had to get out; he was becoming more and more violent with each incident.

"I have to go and make a run, get off the couch, go get in the bed, and get some rest. I will clean this up," he said.

I welcomed the chance to get away from him. I gathered up my pillow and blanket and ran upstairs. I climbed in bed and waited there until I heard him leave out the house. As I lay in bed, I thought about how much things have changed between us in the last year. When we first met, Matthew and I were so in love. We met at a campus party. Kris talked me into going with her because she wanted to run into a guy she liked. We were seniors in high school and had no business being at a college party. I was standing against the wall just people watching and enjoying the music when Matthew came rushing by and bumped into me; spilling beer all over my jacket.

"Oh shit, I'm so sorry," he apologized.

"It's fine. Do you know where the bathroom is?" I asked.

"I can show you. I'm Matt. What's your name?" he asked.

"Brooke."

"Sorry about that Brooke, if you have to dry clean it I will pay for it," he offered.

"I'm sure it will be fine," I responded.

As he led me to the bathroom, I couldn't get over how cute he was. I was never really into white boys, but Matthew had a bit of swag to him that drew me in. Later on, I saw him strolling with some of his frat brothers and it all made sense; he was one of those white boys with soul.

Before the night ended, Matthew found me sitting with Kris and her friend. He asked me to come outside to talk to him. I couldn't resist those blue eyes and perfect smile. He looked like a young replica of the late Paul Walker, simply gorgeous. As we talked, the inevitable question came up...

"So, are you a freshman?" he asked.

"No, I'm a senior," I said, being sarcastic.

"Wow really, I've never seen you around. I'm a sophomore."

"I'm a senior in high school," I said a little embarrassed.

"Oh, that explains it. So, what are you doing at this party?" he asked.

"The same thing you're doing; having a good time."

"I see. How old are you?"

"I will be eighteen in less than two months."

"Really? When is your birthday?" he asked.

"You sure do ask a lot of questions. My birthday is March 24th," I said.

"March 24th? Cool, I'd love to take you out for your birthday."

"Oh really?" I asked.

I knew where he was going with it, so I gave him my number. After we left the party, I didn't see or speak to Matthew again until my birthday. I couldn't believe he called. When I asked my parents if he could take me out, they didn't decline because I was officially 18, but I still had a midnight curfew. I was on cloud nine, I was graduating in two months and I was already accepted into the same college as Matthew. After that night on my birthday, Matthew and I have been inseparable. He was so sweet and caring back then but now, he was monster.

I heard him start up his car and I listened to the sound of his car leaving our driveway before I got out of the bed and took a quick shower. I needed to get dressed and catch up with Kris. Then I planned to meet Bianca at the house to break the news to Brianna about Kevin and Dee. I made a note to be back in time to cook dinner for Matt. He's been coming in pretty late lately, so I knew I had more than enough time to get things straight for my sister.

Before I got in the shower, I called Kris. "Hello," she answered.

"Hey girl, you ok?" I asked, she sounded like she had been crying.

"Yeah, I'm ok. I'm just waking up and about to ice my hand. It's still throbbing from last night."

"I bet, Tyson. Hey, you think you can meet me at the house? I feel like we should all be there to break the news to Bri. Bianca should be on her way back from the Chi as we speak."

"Yeah of course; I will meet you there."

"Ok, see you later. Love you."

"Love you too."

We hung up and I got ready to start what seemed like would be a very long day.

Brianna

As the sun shined through the huge bay window in my room, I woke up with a smile and a familiar smell of Dolce and Gabbana's *The One*, filled my nostrils. I turned over to face the handsome man lying next to me, Harley. He looked so peaceful laying there, his dreads falling carelessly around his face. I moved a few to get a better look at his face. He reached up and took my hand in his, brought it to his lips and kissed my palm.

"Good morning Gorgeous," he said.

"You're a light sleeper".

"I felt you watching me. What's on your mind?" he asked.

"Nothing, I'm just admiring the view".

"Come here," he said, as he pulled me closer. I laid my head on his chest. I could hear his heart beating strong, and steady. As I played with his locs I said, "Thank you for coming back last night."

"No problem Gorgeous. I told you last night that I'm here for you. Whenever, and whatever you need," he responded.

All I could do was smile. This man had me mesmerized. For a moment, I was lost in his words, in his scent, in his presence. I felt so comfortable with him. Last night, he didn't come expecting anything, he just held me, and we talked. It was nice. No pressure, the sexual tension was there, but I didn't feel obligated to act on it. He agreed to stay the night with me. When we came upstairs to the room, he got comfortable in his briefs and T-shirt and I changed into shorts and a tank top. We just laid together and talked until we fell asleep.

This morning was a different story. This morning my body ached for him to touch me with his strong hands. I wanted to be wrapped in the strength of his toned arms, and I wanted those same soft lips that kissed the palm of my hand to kiss places that haven't been touched in weeks. As I lay on his chest, I could feel that he wanted the same thing. I knew because I had a third leg growing against my hip. I ran my fingers down his shoulders and down the length of his arm as he stroked my hair. He lifted up and kissed me on the forehead. I asked, "Are you hungry?"

"Starving," he responded, as he lifted me up by my waist forcing me to straddle him. He sat up with me on his lap, and gently laid me back on the bed. Now he was on top. He kissed me, and waited. I kissed him back, my way of giving him permission to continue. He lifted my tank top over my head and began to kiss my breast. My body was on fire. I wanted this, but part of me felt like it was all happening too soon. That part of me caused me to blurt out insane questions like, "I thought you were hungry?"

"I am," he responded, and then removed my shorts. Seconds later, those same beautiful, full, soft lips that kissed my palm, were now kissing my lower lips. Between kisses, he licked my swollen clit. Kiss…lick…kiss…lick. The rhythm went on and on until he eventually just settled on my clit. Lick, lick, lick, lick. With each stroke, I felt my head spinning more and more. I began to pull at his locks, keeping him in place, it was so perfect, and he worked my clit so perfect. I was afraid to let him move. I was afraid to breath and lose my position. I held my breath, I held on to it until I began to feel lightheaded. I felt my body about to explode into a thousand little pieces. My abdominal muscles getting tight, the grip on his locks getting stronger. He wouldn't let up, only to say "Breath baby, just breath."

The sound of his voice sent me over the edge; I exhaled loudly, and let my climax take over. I threw my head back into the pillows, closed my eyes and rode that orgasmic wave as Harley sucked to catch every drop of my release. I've waited so long to release this tension, and as Harley came up for air, covered in my honey, I felt a little embarrassed. However, the look on his face told me he was surprised and he liked it.

"Damn baby," he said, with a smile.

He made his way back up, trailing kisses along the way until he found my upper lips, panting and moist from me biting while he had breakfast. Just when I caught my breath, he took it away again with a deep, passionate kiss. It lasted long enough for me to get my second wind, and I was ready to return the favor. As we kissed, I lifted up slightly urging him to roll over. It was my turn to be in control. As he rolled over, he lifted me with him, never breaking our kiss. His strength turned me on.

Once on top, I went right to work. I started with soft kisses around his neck, nibbled on his ear a bit. Light moans escaped him as I kissed and licked his collarbone. I planted soft kisses down his chest and licked around his abs. the further I went down, the more erratic his breathing became, the more turned on I was. I looked up at him, his eyes were closed, his mouth was open, and I never stopped licking. I tugged on his briefs, freeing that third leg that was begging to be released. He opened his eyes, and I felt him watching me.

First, I kissed the head, soft slow kisses. Ran my tongue around the tip, and sucked lightly. I moved my tongue in circles. As I sucked, I felt him grab my head and thrust deeper into my throat. I pulled back, not done teasing him yet. I licked his shaft from top to bottom, kissed its length. I deep throated him, long enough to make him moist. I heard him moan, "Shittt." That gave me the motivation to keep going. His third leg, wet with my saliva, I gripped it lightly and stroked it up and down as I tickled his balls with my tongue. "Oh shit, damn baby," he said, but I didn't stop there. I continued to stroke as I pulled both balls into my mouth and caressed them with my tongue.

By now, Harley was breathing hard and pulling at my locs. First, he would pull hard and realize he was pulling too tight then loosen up. I was so turned on by his response, that I ended my tease. I took him into my mouth, made sure that I took all of him as deep as I could. I wanted him to hit that G-spot in the back of my throat. I took him deep, and then pulled him out. I continued this motion as his fingers intertwined with my locs and he began to moan obscenities. I continued until he couldn't take it anymore and tried to pull away. I sucked harder, and he pulled some more. So, I

120

sucked harder and finally lost the battle as he pulled and lifted me up on top of him. I opened my legs wide to straddle him, as he placed me on his third leg, perfect position to hit my other G-spot.

I rocked my hips, held on to his chest, and threw my head back while my mouth opened to an 'O'. At first his girth and length was too much for me to take, he made me feel like a virgin all over again. I was so wet that it made it easier for him to glide in and out of me. I continued to rock until my body took form. Once I was adjusted, I wined on him moving my hips in a circular motion and rocking back hard. His hands were on my waist guiding me, and moved to my ass and grabbed it. I leaned forward, and started to bounce on him; he grabbed my ass tighter and began to slap it. It hurt so good, I let out a slight moan.

I kissed him. I kissed him like I was begging for mercy, as he lifted up and pounded into me while I dropped it onto him. It hurt so good. I slowed my wine down, to catch my breath.

"You ok? You want me to stop?" he asked, still grinding into me.

"No, please, don't stop," I responded.

He picked me up and rolled me onto my back. As he entered me again, we looked into each other's eyes, no words were said, and none needed to be said. At that moment, we connected, on another level. I closed my eyes to enjoy the ride. Soft kisses fell on my closed eyelids, on my nose, my forehead, and then my cheeks. He licked my neck, and behind my ear, down to my collarbone all the while still grinding. I rubbed his strong back, felt every muscle contract and release as he grinded into me. I slid my hands down to his ass and pushed him deeper inside me. I wrapped my legs around his waist and pushed him deeper. I was on the verge of coming.

He kept the same pace, push then grind, push then grind, as I rolled my hips. He was there, on my spot. He stayed there, I rolled my hips and he grabbed me and stopped me. He continued, push, and grind, push and grind. "Baby, I'm about to cum," I said.

"Me too, cum with me baby, cum with me," he moaned.

Push and grind, push and grind. I held him closer. I held on tight as my orgasm took control of me. He came, hard, and loud. The final thrust sending me into a fog. We laid there panting, sweaty, and satisfied. He rolled over onto his back, and pulled me closer to him. He whispered in my ear, "You know this means we go together right?" I laughed; he was so funny and random. I responded with a kiss, and rolled over to my side with my butt against his now soft, but still impressive, third leg and his arm around my waist. We drifted off to sleep.

Moments later, we were startled awake by my big sister barging into my bedroom with Krystal on her heels.

"Damn, sorry B," Brooke said embarrassed, and then pushed Kris out the door with her.

I was so embarrassed. I was grown, but it was something about having my big sister walk in on me in bed naked with I guess, my new man, whom she hadn't even met.

"Oh shit," I said aloud.

"You want me to go?" Harley asked.

"No, stay and just get dressed. I need to introduce you to my sister," I said. I kissed him, and went into the bathroom to clean up.

Harley came in behind me and kissed me on my neck. I handed him a towel and we stepped into the shower together to clean ourselves up as evidence of this morning's activities rolled down my leg. After cleaning each other up, we headed downstairs to face the music. Evidently, Kris had already filled Brooke in.

"So, this is Harley? I'm Brooke, nice to finally meet you," she said sarcastically, while eyeing me.

"Call me Ryder. It's nice to meet you Brooke," Harley responded.

"Hi Ryder," Kris said.

"What's up Kris?" he responded.

I interrupted the little game Brooke was about to play. "So, what's going on? Why y'all kicking down doors and taking names?" I asked.

"We came over to talk to you. I'm sorry, we didn't know you had company," Brooke responded.

"It's cool, I'm about to make something to eat. Are y'all hungry?" I asked. They looked like they were getting comfortable and weren't leaving anytime soon anyway.

"Yeah, can you make us some potato balls?" Brooke asked. She always wanted my potato balls, but she would have to wait for dinner.

"I was thinking more on the line of cold cuts. We could save that for dinner. Potatoes and grilled salmon sound good for later?" I asked.

"Sounds good to me," said Kris.

I looked over at Brooke. "I guess," she responded. I swear, sometimes I couldn't tell which one of us was the oldest. She was so darn spoiled. I headed to the kitchen with Harley right behind me.

"Hey Gorgeous, I'm gonna head out and let you kick it with your sisters," he said.

"You sure you don't want to eat first?" I asked.

"Yeah, stay and have lunch with us," Brooke butted in.

Harley smiled and said, "Nah, y'all got it, but I will be back later for those potatoes." He winked at me. I walked him to the door and kissed him goodbye, promising to call him later, before I started dinner. I walked back into the kitchen ready to grill my sisters on the real reason why they came busting in my room.

"Damn girl, you move fast," joked Kris.

I ignored her and stated, "Alright heffas, speak."

"Girl, he is fine!" Brooke said. Kris and I busted out laughing.

"For real, y'all what's going on?" I asked.

Brooke started to speak, and was interrupted by Bianca coming through the front door. She came into the kitchen and stood next to Kris.

"Damn, y'all told her already?" she asked.

"Told me what?" I asked.

"Not yet, you right on time," Brooke responded.

"On time for what? Somebody better start talking," I said and looked each of them in the eyes.

The room was silent, and no one looked as if they wanted to speak. After a while, Kris broke the silence. "Bri, sit down," she said.

I did as I was told, asking, "What's going on?"

Kris started, "Actually, all of y'all should sit down." Brooke and Bianca followed suit. Kris continued, "Before I go into the reason why we are all here, I have to tell y'all something, so that all of this makes sense. I hope y'all don't look at me differently or get mad at me for not telling you sooner, but I was just scared, and didn't know what you all would say." She began rambling.

Bianca not being the most patient person said, "Girl, stop it with all the dramatics and spit it out."

"Shut up B!" Kris responded. Then she said, "Dee and I have been seeing each other since the before Kevin's grand opening of the new club."

She just blurted it out. She said it and exhaled, then waited. I guess she was waiting for a response from us, and honestly, I didn't know what to say, so I said nothing.

Bianca said, "Oh shit! "

Brooke just sat there, just as dumbfounded as me. Kris looked at her.

"Are you ok? Say something," she said.

"Yeah, I'm just a little surprised. It's not a big deal, but I am shocked," Brooke said

"Me too," I added.

"So, that's why you popped off on her last night! Dayumm it all makes sense now," Bianca said. It sounded like she was sort of laughing when she said it.

"What happened last night?" I asked.

"Well..." Kris began again. "I stopped by the club when I left here because I saw Kevin sitting outside of the house. I wanted to make sure he didn't tell Dee anything crazy about Ryder and Jason coming by."

"Wait, so Kevin knew and we didn't!?" interrupted Brooke.

"That's beside the point, but yes. He caught us in her office a while back. May I continue please?" Kris asked with much attitude.

"Yeah, whatever, BFF," said Brooke.

Kris gave her a side eyed look like she wanted to say something, but decided against it. I just sat, waiting to hear what she had to say.

Kris continued, "Well, when I got to the club and went to Dee office, she wasn't in there, so I went to Kevin's office to see if he had told her anything and..." She paused.

"And what Kris!" I yelled, already knowing where this was going, but I needed to hear her say it. "Kris and what?" I said again.

"And, I found him and Dee fucking on the chair behind his desk." She started to cry, but continued talking. "I lost it, after that I just remember me hitting and hitting her. Kevin tried breaking it up but couldn't and I eventually got dragged out by Big E and Seth," she finished. Still crying, she said, "I'm sorry B, but Kevin and Dee is foul for that shit."

I didn't know what to say. All of this time, I wanted to know who ruined my life, and now that I knew, I didn't know what to do or say. Surprisingly enough, I wasn't angry, and I didn't have a sudden urge to hurt Dee or Kevin. Once again, I was numb.

As Brooke comforted Kris, Bianca walked over to me and asked me what I wanted to do. I loved my sister, she was always ready for whatever, but I didn't have anything for her.

"I think I'm gonna go lay down," I said. I turned to Kris, "Kris, I'm sorry. I can tell you really cared about her." I walked out the kitchen and up to my room, confused.

Chapter Six

Bianca

I couldn't believe Bri was just letting that shit go like that. There is no way that I would just let that ride. Dee knew that Kevin and Bri were together and getting married, and she still slept with him; all the while, fucking Kris too. That's a scandalous bitch for you. If you ask me, they both deserve to be fucked up.

"So that's it? We're just gone let them fuck over my sisters and get away with it? Please tell me y'all got a plan or something!" I yelled.

I hated seeing my sister so hurt. And Kris, she broke down crying over that bitch. It broke my heart and now I was seeing red. If they didn't make up their minds to do something about it, I was gonna make some phone calls myself.

"Calm down Bianca, let's think about this. Bri checked out, let's just give her some time to think through this and we can figure this all out together later. Right now, I think we should go up and check on her though. She shouldn't be alone, and Kris you need to lay down too," Brooke said.

We all went upstairs to Bri's room, but she wasn't in there. I walked down to our parents' old room, and found her in their California King bed crying her eyes out. I knew she would be in there, I knew she needed our mom. We all climbed in bed with her and held each other. I listened to my sisters cry themselves to sleep, and made up my mind that Kevin and Dee had to pay.

We were all napping peacefully until I heard a loud banging on our front door. I jumped up startled. "Who the fuck is that?" I asked.

We all got up and headed down stairs to see who was at the door. As we got closer, I noticed that it was the cops. "Oh shit! Kris did you kill the bitch?" I asked.

"I…I don't know. I can't go to jail," Kris started crying.

I opened the door for the officers. "Hi can I help you?" I said.

"Yes, and you are?" the overweight lady cop asked.

"Bianca Williams, I live here."

"Ms. Williams, is there a Krystal Evans here?"

Krystal appeared from behind me, "Yes, that's me can I help you?" she asked.

"Krystal Evans, you are under arrest. You have the right to remain silent, anything you say can and will be used against you in the court of law…" the lady cop went on and on as Kris was handcuffed and practically carried to the police car. I looked back at my sisters and yelled, "Go get my phone from upstairs, now!"

We stood and watched as Kris was carried away, shocked out of our minds. I watched them as the officers placed her in the car and closed the door. Brooke and Brianna were crying. I told Brianna again to go grab my phone. I needed to make some calls to help Kris.

Kevin

I looked her over; she had two black eyes, fractured ribs, and multiple stitches in her swollen lip and a mild concussion. Dee was fucked up, and Kris had a hell of a right hook. I watched Dee lying in the hospital bed with a scowl on her face as the doctor poked and prodded at her. She had to stay in the hospital overnight for observation, but she was being released today. "The pain from your fractures will last a few weeks; you can expect to have some problems getting around. I suggest you stay in bed and rest until you are strong enough to move around on your own. I am prescribing you some pretty heavy pain medication, which will cause drowsiness, so no drinking or driving while you're taking these. Okay?" the doctor asked.

Dee nodded, and winced probably from the pain of moving her head.

"Any questions?" he asked.

"No," Dee whispered.

"Ok, feel better Ms. Phillips" he said. And with that, he rushed out the room probably to the next patient in need of his care. We were both silent as we stared at each other for a moment. I started to say something but the nurse walked in to help her into a wheel chair. I watched as she struggled and screwed her face up in pain as she climbed off the bed and into the chair. No words were said as I followed behind them to the emergency room exit.

"I will go pull the car around," I said and left out to the parking lot. Once I pulled up, I opened the passenger door, and helped Dee get inside of the car. I felt bad for her, but really, I just wanted to get her home and in bed, so I can head over to talk to Bri. I know she knew about us by now. I know it wouldn't be the smartest thing to do, but I had to talk to her. She deserved to hear it from me.

As I pulled away from the hospital, I glanced over at Dee to see her crying. I started to ask her if she was ok, but decided against it. So we rode in silence. We stopped to fill her prescription at the pharmacy before heading to her place. A twenty-minute drive felt like hours. I pulled into her driveway and she handed me her house keys. I ran up, unlocked the door and pushed it open. I went back to help her out the car, and grab her things. She headed inside to the back of the house to her bedroom and I followed behind with her bags. I placed the bags at the foot of the bed and placed the pills on her nightstand. I was walking out the bedroom when she sat on the bed and asked me, "Are you on your way to go see her?"

"Huh, who?" I asked.

"Don't play dumb with me?" she said and the tears started again.

"Yes," I said, and awaited her response.

She was silent for a moment.

"You never loved me did you?" she asked.

I hesitated. For a moment, I considered spinning her question, but I felt I should start being honest with her.

"Yes, I always loved you. But I was never in love with you," I said.

"I knew it. I just didn't want to admit it. Kris. Kris loved me. And I couldn't accept it because I was so stuck on you," she cried.

It was time for me to leave. I turned around and continued out the door. She didn't try to stop me this time with more questions. I was fine with that. We both needed to move on, which is why I decided not to go see Bri. I figured I would wait a few days for all of this to cool down. Instead, I went to the club to clean up my office and get some paperwork done. I still hadn't completed the payroll yet.

A few hours into getting some work done, my cell phone rings. Unknown number, it had to be Dee. At first, I was going to ignore it, but I decided to go ahead and hear her out. She probably wanted to cry her heart out to me again and beg me to come back over to her place.

"Yeah," I answered unenthusiastically. Except it wasn't Dee.

"Hi, is this Kevin Jackson?" asked the unfamiliar voice.

"Yes. Who is this?" I asked.

"Mr. Jackson, this is Dr. Futrell at St. Mary's Hospital. I'm sorry to disturb you at this hour. But do you know Deanna Phillips? She has you down as her emergency contact," she asked.

"Yes, she's my friend," I said. "Why?"

"I'm sorry sir, but there has been an accident. We need you to come to the hospital?"

"Accident! What kind of accident? Is Dee ok?" I asked in a panic.

"Sir, please. Can you make it to the hospital tonight?" she asked again.

"I'm on my way," I said and hung up.

I got into my car and drove as fast as I could to the hospital. I'm sure I got there in record time. So many thoughts were racing through my mind on my way there. What kind of accident? Was Dee ok? I ran inside and immediately asked for Dr. Futrell. They paged her and she came up front right away.

"Mr. Jackson, thank you for coming. Ms. Phillips was brought in about two hours ago by paramedics. She has overdosed on pain medication. According to the paramedics who brought her in, she dialed 911 before she passed out."

"Damn!" I yelled. I couldn't believe what I was hearing. Dee tried to take herself out.

The startled doctor waited as I collected myself, before she continued. "We were able to remove the pills from her stomach. She's sleeping now, but she is on suicide watch." She asked, "Mr. Jackson, how long have you known Ms. Philips? Has she ever tried committing suicide before?"

I didn't answer her right away; I was still in shock. "No, not that I know of," I said.

"Has anything changed in her life recently?" she asked.

"Can I see her?" I asked. Not wanting to answer her questions.

"Sure, follow me Mr. Jackson," she said.

When we got to the room, the doctor did not say anything. She left us alone and walked out closing the door behind her. I walked over to the bed and looked at Dee. I was trying to understand why she would do some shit like this. I touched her forehead and she shifted a bit. I heard her whisper, "Kris." I hated seeing her like this. I kissed her on the forehead and walked out of the room.

I reached into my pocket to make a phone call and noticed I had a text message from Bianca.

Bianca: *So your side bitch not only fucks my sister's fiancé, buts she also fucks over my friend AND gets her thrown in jail?! Tell that bitch to watch her back! If my sis don't get released on Monday, I'm coming for that ass!*

This bitch has really lost her mind. What is she talking about? Kris is in jail? I looked through the small window in the door, into the room where Dee was resting. She looked so sad, and weak. Maybe that's what caused her to try to take herself out, the guilt from pressing charges on Kris. She must've talked to the police after I dropped her off at home. The way she was calling out to Kris, I knew she wouldn't follow through on the charges.

This was just all too much for me to deal with right now. Bianca and her empty threats, Dee and Kris' drama. I needed to focus on getting my woman back. I decided not to go back in the room, I had to get home and get my head straight. I needed to talk to Brianna. I had to make her listen to me. I love her, but I fucked up…again. Seeing her with that other dude fucked me up. She belonged to me; she just didn't know it yet.

Kris
> *I couldn't believe this bitch pressed charges on me! She fucked me over, broke my heart, and ruined my sister's relationship, and now she's the victim, this is some bullshit,* I thought, as I rode silently in the back of the police car. To be honest I was scared shitless, but I was more angry, than anything. Dee got what she deserved; she needed to feel my pain that she caused. Yea, she called me a few times begging and pleading her case, maybe I knocked some sense into her, but I couldn't stand to hear her voice. I told her if she wanted to make me happy, to go kill herself, and do both my sister and I a favor! Was I supposed to feel sorry for putting her ass in the hospital? Hell no!

As we pulled up to the county jail, shit got real. I didn't want to get out of the car but I didn't have a choice. I walked into the cold building and was escorted to a check-in desk where I was finger printed, my mugshot was taken, and I was thrown into a holding cell until Monday morning when I would see a judge. I sat for a while gathering my thoughts, and then I remembered I could make a phone call. I called out to the guard to see if I could get my phone call.

"Hey, can I use the phone?" I asked.

"You didn't get your phone call?" the overweight guard asked, still sitting behind the desk with his feet propped up on top.

"No," I said.

The guard reluctantly got up from his comfy seat and escorted me to a room to make my call. I waited for a while until Brooke picked up,

"Hello?" she answered.

"B, it's me. You gotta get me out of here," I cried.

"I know, I know. Bianca is working on it; she said a lawyer would be down to meet with you in the morning before you go in front of the judge. How are you feeling? They treating you right in there?"

"Yea, I'm in a holding cell by myself, so it's not that bad. I just want to get out of this place. It's cold, it stinks like wet clothes, and it's dirty." I continued to cry.

"I know love, it's just one night and you will be home." Brook tried her best to comfort me.

"Ok. B, I'm so mad right now. I don't know if I'm crying because I'm scared or because I'm ready to go off and explode!" I was so angry. I never been this angry before.

"It's cool Kris, just stay calm, and we will see you in the morning."

"Ok, I love you sis," I said.

"I love you too sis," she said and hung up the phone

I was then escorted back to my cell. I sat on the cold concrete bench and leaned my head against the damp wall. I didn't sleep; I stayed up all night thinking of all the different outcomes that could happen from what I did to Dee. The thought that I should've just killed her came to mind, but then things would be worst. To try to distract myself, I listened to the radio station the guard was listening to, and the music helped to calm my nerves. Time took forever to go by, but before I knew it, the first shift guard was coming to get me, to escort me to the courthouse and talk to my lawyer then see the judge.

Brooke

After the shock of seeing my best friend in handcuffs and taken to jail, telling us she's gay, and Bri finding out Kevin cheated on her with Dee, who is Kris's lover, or ex-lover; I was mentally and physically exhausted. We waited around all day to hear back from Bianca's friend. Apparently, he was an attorney. When did she get an attorney anyway? There are so many secrets surrounding all of us, I didn't know what to do. When did my sisters and I lose that connection? There was a time when we told each other everything.

Somehow, everyone ended up at my place. I needed to get home and start dinner for Matt. We were still waiting to hear back from that attorney. I mean, what was taking him so long anyway? Bianca was in the living room watching TV and Bri was outside talking to Ryder in the car. She called him after Kris was taken into custody. He had a way with her that made me smile for my sister. He relaxed her immediately; I could tell he was going to be good for her. I was in the kitchen chopping vegetables when I heard Matt come storming in the house yelling.

"Brooke!" he yelled.

"I'm in the kitchen, baby. What's wrong?" I asked.

Bianca got up and walked into the kitchen with me, when Matt turned the corner and saw her, his demeanor softened a bit. However, the fire was still in his eyes. I tried to keep it cool.

"Hey baby? What's wrong?" I asked.

"Nothing, what's going on in here?" he asked, probably surprised to see Bianca here with me.

"I'm just getting dinner ready. Are you hungry?" I asked.

"Yea, I'm gonna go up to the room. Call me when it's ready."

"Ok," I responded.

Matt gave me a look that only I noticed because I've seen it many times before. He was angry, and as always, I didn't know why. I was happy to have Bianca there with me in that moment. I was too weak and exhausted to block being hit. When Matt disappeared out of the kitchen, Bianca said something that changed my whole perspective.

"He's been getting high?" she stated more as a statement than a question.

"What do you mean? No, he's not high," I responded.

"Yes he is Brooke; I can see it in his eyes. He's high, I can smell it too," she said.

"Bianca, you don't know what you're talking about. Since when do you know how drugs smell? We are talking about Matthew here. He is the last person that would do drugs," I said.

"B, I'm telling you, Matt is fucked up right now. He has that same look and smell... Never mind, just trust me on this aight?

"B, he's not using. Let it go!" I yelled. In my heart, I knew she was right. That explained everything.

I threw the meat in the oven and walked to the living room to sit on the couch. Bianca and I got caught up in watching *The First 48*, when Ryder and Bri joined us. The attorney had finally called Bianca back. She said he didn't go into any detail, but he said that Kris would have to sit overnight. He said he was confident that she would be released sometime tomorrow, so we still did not know what she was being held for. It wasn't confirmed, but I knew it involved Dee. She probably pressed charges for that well deserved ass whooping she received. Brianna interrupted my thoughts.

"Hey, where is Matt? I wanted to introduce him to Harley," she said.

"He went upstairs to lie down; he will be down when the food is ready," I said.

"Oh ok. I should be doing the same thing, after the day we had."

I know she was upset about the whole Dee and Kevin situation, but she tried her best not to show it. Ryder sat by her side and lightly rubbed her back. That made me miss the affection I used to get from Matt. I decided I would go upstairs and convince him to come down and join us.

When I walked in the room, Matt was coming out the bathroom. "Hey baby, you ok?" I asked.

"Yeah, I'm fine. Is the food done?"

"No, but…" I started, but he cut me off.

"But what? Why are you in here then?"

I was scared. "I just wanted you to come downstairs to join us. Brianna and her new boyfriend are here, and she wants you to meet him," I explained.

He looked at me for a minute. I didn't know what to think or say, so I waited.

"I will be down in a second," he said. He was eerily calm.

"Ok," I said, and left out of the room.

I walked down the stairs and saw Bianca leaving out the door on the phone. I went back to the living room to join Ryder and Bri back on the couch. Moments later, Matt came downstairs cleaned up and surprisingly affectionate. I was thrown by the sudden change of mood. It was nice, but it was hard for me to enjoy it because deep down I knew it was a front. He made small talk with Ryder as Bri and I checked on the food. Bianca eventually came back to join us, but only for a second. She said something came up and she had to leave. She asked Matt to walk her out. I stayed behind and kept Brianna and Ryder entertained.

I decided to do all I could to make Ryder and Brianna stay longer. After we all ate dinner, Bri and I cleaned up the kitchen and decided to start a card game. We played Spades for a few hours, first couples against each other, and then Bri and I beat Matt and Ryder a few times. It was getting late, Bri and Ryder was getting ready to leave. Matt and I walked them out, and I told Bri that I would see her at the house tomorrow.

After they were gone, Matt and I enjoyed another drink. He was still being nice. We went upstairs to the room and decided to take a shower together. While in the shower, he kissed me and said, "You look so beautiful." I didn't know how to respond to that. Matthew hadn't complimented me in a long time, at least not without first apologizing for hitting me. Things were going well, so I relaxed. We shared a few more kisses in the shower, which turned into full, hot, steamy lovemaking. Matthew dropped to his knees and kissed me below my belly, and suckled my clit until my juices mixed with the hot shower water. He then turned me around, stroking me nice and slow from behind.

The hot water from the rainfall showerhead poured onto us. As Matthew stroked me, I gripped the metal towel bar and threw my hips back at him. He held on tight to my waist and lightly bit my shoulder. I could hear him moaning and groaning. He then pulled out and turned me around so that I could face him. He lifted me by my waist and placed me on his hips. He pressed my back against the wall and slid inside of me. My mouth fell open and I let out a sigh of ecstasy. Matthew kissed me and we continued to hold each other as he grinded into me until we both came, together.

After the shower, we went to bed, and he fell fast asleep. Once I knew he was out, I decided to get me some rest too. I don't know what brought on the change in his mood, but I was thanking God, even in my sleep, for sparing me tonight.

Chapter Seven

Kris

"All rise for the Honorable Judge Walter Harris," said the bailiff. I stood up proudly next to my attorney. I knew that I would be going home today. They couldn't hold me without Dee here to testify against me. I looked around the courtroom and saw my sisters, Brianna, Brooke, and Bianca. Brooke and Brianna had worried looks on their faces. From what I heard, I did a serious number on Dee, but I didn't feel bad; she got what she deserved. I looked over at Bianca; she nodded at me, letting me know that I'd be ok. That helped me to relax. Ryder was here too, sitting next to Brianna.

"In the case of People versus Krystal Nicole Evans, docket number 239847, on the charges of felony assault and battery. On these charges how do you plea?" He looked up from the docket and stared at me, urging me to speak.

"Not guilty, Your Honor," I replied.

Then my lawyer stepped in, "Your Honor, based on the fact that the alleged victim failed to show up in court today, and is not here to press charges, I am asking that all charges be dismissed."

"You have a good point Mr. Irving. Ms. Thompson, where is the plaintiff?" Judge Harris asked.

"Your Honor, we have been unable to contact Ms. Phillips this morning. She has not returned our calls," the D.A. responded.

"Very well then, I do not see any reason for us to continue. I hereby drop all charges against Ms.

Evans. Ms. Evans you are free to go," the judge said, and then banged the gavel.

The D.A. stood there looking dumbfounded.

I looked over to my attorney, "Thank you so much," I said.

I looked back at my sisters, and they told me they would meet me outside. After signing a few papers, I walked outside the courtroom and noticed there was some commotion going on by Brianna's truck. I quickly ran over to see Kevin and Harley exchanging words.

"Look, this don't concern you. This is between me and my fiancée," said Kevin.

"Ex fiancée," responded Harley. "Now, she said she didn't want to talk to you, so why don't you do us all a favor and move around."

"Who the fuck do you think you're talking to!" Kevin yelled, stepping closer into Harley's face.

After that, all hell broke loose. Harley reached back and punched Kevin so hard, he lifted off his feet and went tumbling to the ground. Brianna and Bianca ran over to hold Harley back and just as they lead him to the car, I saw Kevin reach into is back and pull out a gun. I screamed, but I wasn't fast enough. Kevin let off two shots, while still on the ground. Police started rushing towards him, one fired his weapon, striking Kevin and for a moment, I was in shock at all I had just witnessed. I was caught in a daze until I heard a blood-curdling scream. I looked over and saw Brianna lying face down in the street, blood streaming out of her back. Then, everything went black.

Brooke

I was in a state of shock. Everything was happening so fast around me, as I held on to my sister. "It's going to be ok, it's going to be ok," I kept repeating. I was attempting to soothe her, but I also needed to tell myself the same thing. My body was shaking uncontrollably, and tears were blinding my vision. I couldn't focus on anything around me; I just needed my sister to be ok. I was still in a fog as the paramedics came on the scene, they forced me to let go of my little sister. I watched as they rushed her onto a gurney and loaded her into the ambulance.

I couldn't move, I just sat there in the street where my sister had just collapsed and I cried. I cried for my sister, I needed her to be ok. I cried as I thought about, how that could have very well been me, and wondered if my husband would even care. I cried, thinking about my parents and how worried they would be about what we were currently going through. I cried, fearing the most tragic outcome of all of this. I needed my sister; I prayed that God wouldn't take her from me.

Bianca came over to me and picked me up off the ground, and walked me to the car. She told me that we had to meet Brianna at the hospital. Kris was in the backseat crying, and Ryder must have ridden with Bri in the ambulance. I could tell that Bianca was shaken up, but I was proud of her for taking control. Usually, I am the one who's in control, level headed during a crisis, but this was different. With all that has been going on, I had finally reached my breaking point.

I don't know how long the ride to the hospital took, but I know we made record time. We came just after the ambulance arrived and found Ryder in the waiting area, banging his head against the wall. When he saw us, he came over and told us that she was being rushed into surgery, and we all had to wait out here. I could see the hurt and anger in his eyes. I hugged him, and told him that everything will be ok; I had to believe that. Bianca and Kris joined in, all of us crying silently, and praying for a positive outcome. Then, Ryder looked at all of us, and said, "I'm gonna kill him." I knew that was a promise and not a threat, from the way he said it. I also knew that if Kevin was shot, he was very likely to have been at this hospital as well.

Everyone was still on edge as we waited, Ryder kept checking with the nurse to find out any progress, but no one would tell us anything. Hours had passed by and we hadn't heard anything from the doctors.

"B, I think we should call mom and dad," said Bianca.

"Yea, I know, I just don't know what to say to them," I said, as I started to tear up again.

We walked over to a quiet area in the waiting room, and Bianca and I made the call together.

"Hey baby girl!" Dad answered.

"Daddy…" I responded trying to hold back from crying.

"What's wrong baby? Are you alright?" he asked.

"Daddy, Brianna…" I couldn't get the words out.

"Brianna what? What's going on?" he asked me. "Deb, pick up the other phone baby, something's wrong," he yelled to my mom.

"Hello? What's going on?" Mom asked.

"Kevin shot Brianna, Mommy and now we are at the hospital. The doctors won't talk to us and tell us anything. You gotta come home mommy, daddy. "Bianca was crying and talking at the same time, her words moving at the speed of light.

"Wait, slow down baby, shot?" Daddy responded.

"We are on our way!" mom yelled.

I could hear my mom crying and it broke my heart. I could also hear the anger, pain, and confusion that both of my parents shared as Bianca and I told Daddy what happened. My mom had gotten off the phone to pack their bags and to check for the next outbound flight to Milwaukee. Meanwhile, Daddy attempted to comfort us, and said a prayer with us for my sister. After praying, we ended the call, looking forward to the comfort of our parents and getting positive news from the doctors.

By now we had been waiting for some kind of update from the doctors for over four hours, when a young, black, female, doctor came into the waiting room looking for the Williams family. She was accompanied by another doctor, an older white guy, so immediately, I prepared for the worst news. Ryder spoke up for everyone.

"Hi, how is she doing? When can I see her?" He asked.

"Hi, Mr.?" The young female doctor asked.

"Ryder," Harley responded.

"Mr. Ryder, I am Dr. Jones. Sorry to keep you all waiting, Ms. Williams has experienced severe injuries from the gunshot wound. The bullet traveled through her body and damaged her left kidney, and parts of her intestines. We were able to retrieve the bullet, but she is also exhibiting some internal bleeding, we are trying to find the source of that bleeding. I brought Dr. Kerns with me; he specializes in blood transfusions. Due to the amount of blood she lost, we are keeping him nearby as a precaution," she explained.

"She can have mine, we are the same blood type, take as much as you want, just please help my sister," I cried.

"I assure you that we are doing everything within our means to help your sister. I will let you know when she is out of surgery," she stated, and then she and the other doctor went back to the operating room. Silence fell over the waiting room area, as we all walked back to our seats; satisfied that we had gotten an update, but still unsure of what the final outcome would be.

As we waited impatiently, my phone started ringing, snapping all of us out of our daze. It was Matthew. I realized that he had no idea what was going on, it didn't occur to me to call him. I know that's sad, right? However, at the moment I could really use the comfort of my husband. I got up to answer my phone as I walked to the vending machines to get more privacy.

"Hey baby, Brianna was…" Before I could finish my sentence, Matthew interrupted me.

"Where are you?" he yelled.

I couldn't deal with his shit right now, so I hung up the phone. Shocked at my own strength, I turned around and walked back to my seat. I was finally done with Matthew, and I made up my mind that it was time for me to leave him for good. Today made me realize that life was too short to live in misery. He called back a few times, and then the calls stopped. I didn't worry about what I had waiting for me when I went back home, and at this point, I didn't care. I shifted my focus back to my sister, as I silently said another prayer for her recovery.

Harley

As I sat in the cold waiting room of the hospital, with each passing minute of not knowing if Brianna would be ok, my heart broke a little more. My faith was wavering and my anger boiled over. I didn't know if I was mad at Kevin for what he did to her, or mad at myself, because I caused it. If I hadn't let my anger get the best of me, she wouldn't be on that operating table right now. Had I held back and just walked away, none of this would be happening.

I couldn't shake the thought, the feeling of knowing that because of my pride and the stupid decision I made to give Kevin what he had coming, I may not ever see Gorgeous smile again. I may never again hear her laugh. I wish it were me instead; I wish I could take her place. I needed her to be ok. It's only been a short while since we've known each other, but I knew I'd never meet another woman with her strength, her resilience, her confidence, and genuine compassion. I wanted her, my mind was already made up. I prayed to God over and over tonight, not to take her from me.

On the inside, although I was falling apart, I continued to pray, and hold on to my faith. While on the outside, I remained strong. Kris, Bianca and Brooke were exhausted, scared, and falling apart; I had to be strong for them. Kris had let her exhaustion consume her, and was now curled in a chair sleeping, Bianca was watching TV, and texting someone. I never know what she is thinking. She kept trying to lighten the mood by cracking jokes about the female nurse behind the desk who had a full 5 o'clock shadow. Brooke was ignoring someone's calls, maybe her husband. I remember Brianna telling me that Brooke and her husband were having problems, she didn't go into any detail, just said she had a feeling. She must have been right because he sure wasn't here showing his concern for his sister in-law.

Another hour went by and we finally got the news we were waiting for. The doctor told us that Brianna was out of surgery and heavily sedated. They were able to find the source and stop the internal bleeding. She had one kidney removed, surgery to repair her intestines, and there was some swelling around her spinal cord. The doctors couldn't tell how serious it was, and stated that once the swelling goes down, she may or may not have trouble walking, but for now, we had to wait and see what happens. I asked if we could see her, and she allowed us all to go back and sit with her.

Nothing could prepare me for what I was about to see. When I walked into the room, my legs got weak as I took in the sight of my beautiful woman lying helpless in the small hospital bed. She was hooked to multiple machines, she had tubes flowing out of her nose, an IV line in her arm, and there were multiple monitors around her bed each beeping and going off at different times. I was never the type to cry, but this hurt me. This hurt me to my core. I had to leave the room to regroup. I walked out into the hall and broke down. I blamed myself for this happening and I knew I couldn't do anything about it. I let myself cry for a while until I heard footsteps coming up behind me.

"Hey, you ok?" asked Brooke.

"This is all of my fault. I never should have hit him. That bullet was meant for me, not her," I said angrily.

"No, you can't blame yourself, Ryder. If anyone is to blame it's Kevin. He shot her, not you."

"I just can't stand to see her like this. I don't know what I would do if I lost her," I said.

"She's going to be ok." Brooke said and she hugged me.

She stayed with me a while, as I regrouped to be next to my lady. I knew I had to be strong and the fact that I broke down like that front of Brooke kind of bothered me. However, I loved Brianna, and if I didn't know before, I definitely knew now. I regained control over my emotions so that I could be strong for her. However, in the back of my mind, I was planning to take Kevin out for good.

I pulled up a chair next to her bed, and sat holding her hand as we all sat quietly starring at the woman we all love and were praying for. We sat in silence for a while before Bianca started telling me stories about the trouble they use to get into as teenagers. I sat and listened to the three of them reminisce about their childhood and all of the mischief they got into, especially after they met Kris. We shared some laughs and swapped stories until the sun came up. The whole time in my mind, I was hoping to share this moment with Brianna and longing to hear her laugh again.

At some point, we all ended up falling asleep, me sitting bedside next to Brianna, still holding her hand with my head rested on the bed next to her. Bianca and Kris shared a recliner, and Brooke curled up in a makeshift bed made from two chairs. We were all tired and sleeping awkwardly when we were awakened by the cry of a woman's voice entering the room. Brianna's parents had finally arrived.

Bianca

"Mommy!" I yelled, as I jumped up and ran to greet my parents. I was so excited to see them, I really needed them right now; we all did. I hugged and held on to my mom, and watched my daddy as he walked over to Brianna. I watched him as he examined all of the hospital equipment, taking in the sight of his wounded daughter. The room was silent as we watched my father place his hand on my sister's forehead, and prayed over her. As we watched, my mother began to cry. The sight of my mother crying brought tears to my eyes.

"No, don't start that Deb. No more crying," my father stated. "It's in God's hands now, she will be just fine." Then, he turned to Ryder, "Hi son, what's your name?" he asked.

"Hello sir, my name is Harley Ryder; I'm a friend of Brianna's. I'm so sorry about what happened to your daughter, Sir. I blame myself," Ryder responded, visibly hurt by all that happened.

"Harley, why don't you come with me to go find the doctors? I have some questions for them," my dad responded.

I knew that my dad wanted to talk to him, get to know him, and most importantly find out what happened. I'm sure the story we told him on the phone was probably unclear. I was surprised to hear that Harley blamed himself for what happened. He wasn't the one who shot her, Kevin was, and Kevin was going to pay. However, for now, I had to focus on my sister and making sure that she would recover.

My dad and Ryder had been gone for quite some time, and in the meantime my sisters and I took the time to update my mom on Ryder and give her the full story as to what happened with Kevin. Needless to say, she wasn't surprised to hear that he was back to his cheating ways, but she was surprised that he was so violent and owned a gun. I had to agree with her on that. To be honest, I always thought Kevin was a square. Yeah he played tough and talked a lot of smack, but I always pictured him to be the type to wave a gun, but not pull the trigger. I guess I was wrong.

When we told the story, we left out the part about Kris being a lesbian, her beating Dee up and having to go to court, which is where all of this went down.

"So…" my mom asked. "Where's Kevin now?"

"I think he's somewhere in this hospital. The police shot him; I don't know how serious he was injured. He might even be off to jail by now," I responded.

"Good. I hope they put that boy under the jail for what he did to my baby," my mom said.

"Me too," I replied.

Just then, my dad and Ryder came back to the room. He told my mom basically the same thing the doctor told us about Brianna's condition. My parents hadn't had a chance to rest since they came straight from the airport to the hospital. Brianna was still sedated, so I figured it would be a good time to get them to the house and we could get some rest, and then return to the hospital later.

"Hey mommy and daddy, why don't I take you to the house so you can get some rest? Y'all had a pretty long flight," I said.

"No baby, I will stay right here. You all have been here all night. I can still see your sister's blood on your clothes. Why don't you go clean yourselves up and get some rest. Take your mother with you. I will stay until you all come back," my dad replied.

"You call me if anything changes Bryant," my mother demanded.

"Of course I will baby," he replied.

We all gathered our things until I realized, I drove Ryder's car to the hospital since he rode with Brianna in the ambulance.

"We can't leave without a car." I laughed at my own joke.

"Take mine, I'm staying," Ryder said.

"Son, you should really go home and get some rest," my father replied.

"I'm sorry Sir, but I can't leave her here like this. I have to stay." Then Ryder gave me his keys.

As we were leaving out of the door, I watched Ryder take his seat next to Brianna's bed and hold her hand, as he did the entire night. While walking down the hall to exit through the emergency room, my mom asked Brooke about Matthew's whereabouts and why wasn't he at the hospital with her. Brooke shrugged her shoulders and stated very nonchalantly, "I'm divorcing Matthew." A response that shocked us all.

Kevin

I sat in the hospital bed still a little foggy from the sedative they gave me to retrieve the bullet from my shoulder. I looked around and tried to lift myself up, but the pain for my shoulder wound made it impossible to move. I stopped struggling and just laid there. As I sat back and closed my eyes, a replay of yesterday's event came rushing back to me and I wished that I was back under sedation. I couldn't believe that I had shot Brianna. The guilt of what I had done was too much for me and found myself in excruciating pain. I pressed the button to call my nurse, as I needed some pain medication. The pain from hurting the woman that I loved was too much to bear. Those bullets weren't meant for her. I never meant to hurt her.

When the nurse came in, I explained to her that I was in pain, and she told me she would be back with some pain medicine. All of the IVs were already removed from me, I was about to be released from the hospital and sent to jail. There was a huge, bulky, white officer waiting on the other side of the door to take me in custody. I wondered if he was the one who shot me. If so, I wish he would've killed me. I didn't deserve to live. I needed to know how Brianna was doing.

"Excuse me officer, officer," I called out.

"What?" he asked with much attitude

"Can you tell me if Brianna is ok?"

"Brianna who?" he asked.

"Brianna Williams, the woman I shot by…"
I started to say it was an accident, but he cut me off.

"What? Look, why don't you hold on to your confession until we make it to the precinct," he stated.

The doctor came in and provided me with my medical release papers, and as if on cue, the big officer came in and read me my rights. The pain medication I was promised earlier never came and my shoulder was on fire. I was told that I would receive my pain meds after my statement was taken. The officer was kind enough not to put me in cuffs, as he guided me out the hospital and to the awaiting squad car.

As we pulled off, I noticed Bianca, Brooke and their mother walking out of the hospital. They didn't see me, but the looks on their faces, and all the blood on Brooke's clothes left and eerie feeling in my heart. I said a silent prayer for Brianna, and prepared to take on whatever was coming to me. I deserved it.

Chapter Eight

Brooke

After seeing my sister lying in the street surrounded in a pool of blood, I realized that life was too short. As she laid there on the hard concrete, motionless and fighting for her life, I imagined what life would be like without her and I couldn't bare it. I thought about how my sisters would cope if I were gone. I never want them to experience the pain that I felt yesterday, while holding on to Bri. And that's exactly what would happen, if I did not leave Matthew. I knew he would kill me.

These were the thoughts that ran through my mind as I sat in the back seat of Harley's SUV. I imagined how Matthew would react when I told him I was leaving him. I even considered not telling him at all, and just leaving everything behind. I was terrified to go home. So, when my sister asked me if I wanted to be dropped off at home, I told her no, and asked if I could just borrow something of hers to change into.

Matthew had been calling my phone non-stop all night, then suddenly the calls just stopped. He hadn't called me at all today, and that was bad sign. I knew he was home fuming, just waiting to tear me apart. I knew I wouldn't survive another beating, and something told me this one would be the worst. I was too weak. I hadn't had a decent night's sleep in months for fear of what he might do to me. I was stressing about my sister, I hadn't eaten; I was in no shape to fight off Matthew. I decided to stay where I was safe, at my parents' house.

My mother remained silent the whole way home. I knew she was exhausted, we all were. When I told Bianca not to take me home, I saw my mother began to object, but then she just leaned back and closed her eyes. She probably thought it was best to leave well enough alone, for now. I knew my mother, and she didn't hold her tongue for long. I knew eventually, I'd have to share my horrors with her; however, right now, she had bigger issues to deal with, like praying for my sister's recovery.

Once we arrived at the house, Kris decided she would go home, rest, and then meet us at the hospital later. After seeing her off, I went inside to help mom get settled and talk to Bianca about my plans with Matthew. When I walked in the house, mom was looking around like it was her first time there.

"I see much hasn't changed here. That's good," she said.

Bianca and I just looked at her and ignored her comment. Knowing my mother, she expected things to be in disarray. It was a good thing that Brianna moved back in when she did, because Bianca wasn't the most domestic person.

I helped my mom carry her things upstairs to her room and made sure she had everything she needed before joining Bianca downstairs in the kitchen. She was removing the alcohol out of the cabinets and the fridge in order to take it down to the basement where my parents wouldn't see it. We were grown, but we still didn't want our parents to see us with alcohol. I helped her get everything put up, and we went to her room to get a change of clothes.

"Are you sleepy?" I asked as I grabbed a t-shirt and shorts out of her drawer.

"Not really. Why?" she asked.

"I wanted to see if you would come to my house with me," I said.

"B, I asked you if you wanted me to drop you off, you said no!" Bianca responded, clearly irritated with me.

I was so emotional that I started crying. This caught her off guard. At first, she just looked at me and then she asked, "Are you ok B? What's going on?"

"I just need you to come with me. I don't want to go by myself," I cried. Bianca still didn't understand, so I stood up and lifted my shirt, revealing scars and dark bruises from the last time Matthew kicked me in the stomach after calling me an infertile bitch. A Toys R Us commercial is what set him off that night. The crazy thing was, I went to a fertility doctor and I found out that it wasn't me who was infertile, it was him. Of course, I couldn't tell him that.

"That punk mutha…he hit you?" Bianca raged.

I just started crying harder. "You have to be right when you said he was getting high, I don't know who he is anymore. I can't live like this B," I cried.

Bianca grabbed her gun and told me to get dressed so we can go get my stuff. I did as I was told and went to my room to shower. When I was walking out the door, Bianca was making a phone call.

"Hello, Josh? Hey baby, I need you to meet me somewhere." I heard her say

When Bianca and I pulled up to my house, a black Tahoe was blocking my driveway. "Pull up behind Josh's truck," Bianca said.

I parked the car and proceeded to the front door. Bianca stopped at the truck to talk to Josh and what looked to be three or four other guys in the truck. She and Josh walked into the house with me. I knew Matthew was there because his car was parked in the garage next to mine, and the garage door was up. The downstairs T.V. was on ESPN and empty beer bottles were scattered around the coffee table. I called out, "Matthew, you here?" No answer.

We walked upstairs; I led the way to our bedroom. Bianca and Josh stayed behind in the hall in case Matthew wasn't decent, but when I walked into the room, I didn't see him. I called out again, "Matt?" Bianca and Josh walked into the room. The bathroom door was slightly opened and I pushed it back unprepared for what I was about to see; I screamed in horror.

Seconds later, three guys came running into the room, guns drawn. "It's cool, it's cool," Josh yelled at his friends. Matthew lay unconscious in a puddle of his own urine with a needle sticking out from between his toes.

"Aye yo, that's White Boy!" One of Josh's friends said.

Bianca looked back at him. "I thought I told you he was cut off!" she raged.

"B, he ain't get shit from me. Maybe he copped from one of them Southside niggas, but he didn't get shit from me," he stated.

I couldn't believe what I was hearing, this whole time Bianca knew Matt was doing heroin. I focused back on Matthew, and checked for a pulse. My hands were shaking and I couldn't feel anything. Bianca moved me out of the way and checked for a pulse. "He's still alive. Bug call 911. Josh, help me get him in the shower," she ordered.

While the cold water showered on his head, Bianca kept slapping Matthew in the face. He started to come to, but he was delirious. It didn't take long for the paramedics to arrive. They asked a few questions about Matthew and his health. They also asked about his drug addiction.

"Mrs. Reed, do you know how long he's been out?" the medic asked.

"No," I answered.

"Do you know how long he's been using heroin?" he asked.

"Ask her," I responded, pointing to Bianca, and retreated downstairs to the living room.

They took Matthew to the hospital; I decided not to go with him. I needed some time alone. Josh and his friends left and Bianca sat on the couch watching me clean up Matt's mess.

"B, sit down so I can talk to you please."

I kept cleaning. Bianca, not being one to take a hint, continued to talk anyway.

"B, I didn't know Matt was using until I saw him the night Kris was arrested and I told you he was using. Why are you mad at me?" she asked.

"A lot of this shit don't make sense Bianca. How the hell do you know how somebody look when they high? How did Josh friend know my husband? How did you know he was selling heroin to my husband?" I asked so many questions, and that last question tore me apart. My husband was a heroin addict.

Bianca

It was time for me to come clean to my big sister about my lifestyle and what I have been doing for the past two years since I met Josh. I thought back to the day that I met him. *It was finals week and I was so ready to start my summer break. It was pretty warm outside, so I decided to stop for ice cream. While waiting for my order number to be called, I noticed a black Chevy Tahoe pull into the parking lot. Out stepped Josh and I didn't know them at the time, but Bug and Jay were with him. My order was called, so I walked up to the window and retrieved my ice cream. As I was leaving out, Josh and his boys were coming inside.*

"Excuse me," I said.

"Oh sorry, let me get that for you," Josh replied as he held the door open and stepped back for me to walk through.

"Thank you," I said, and I kept walking.

"Hold up a minute. Can I talk to you for a second?" Josh asked.

His friends walked inside. I stopped and leaned up against my car. He asked, "What's your name?"

"Bianca."

"Hi Bianca, my name is Josh, nice to meet you," he said.

"It's nice to meet you too Josh," I said as I started to eat my ice cream

We made small talk; I don't remember what about because I was too distracted with how fine he was. He stood about six feet tall; he had a slim athletic build like he played basketball or something. He had dark, smooth, chocolate skin and a full beard. His hair was cut low, but I could tell that if he grew it out it would be full of curls, by the wavy texture. I could tell that he was a little arrogant, but it was attractive. He was well-dressed, clean cut, and he smelled good enough to eat. I found myself getting caught up and almost forgot I had a date to get ready for, so I cut things short.

"Look I don't mean to be rude, but I gotta go. I have plans," I said.

"Well, why don't we exchange numbers, maybe I can take you out later tonight?" he asked.

"Can't, I already have a date," I stated.

"Cancel it," he said.

I laughed and continued to get into my car, and he asked, "So you're not gonna give me your number?"

I gave him my number and drove off. He called me before I left the parking lot and we talked all the way, until I got home. Needless to say, I ended up canceling my date that night and hanging out with Josh.

I stopped reminiscing about meeting Josh in my head, and turned my focus to Brooke, by this time she had finished cleaning up the mess Matt made, and sat down next to me on the couch. After getting her to calm down, I explained everything, starting from when I first met Josh.

I told her about how it all started off friendly. I cancelled my date I had that night and hung out in Chicago with Josh. He had a friend that owned a nightclub and he definitely showed us

174

a good time. I mean we were popping bottles left and right, the music was bumping, and Josh actually kept up with me on the dance floor. As attractive Josh was, I knew I couldn't be with him like that, there were way too many women flocking over him and he seemed to know each one of them personally. I wasn't the jealous or hating type, so I let him do his thing.

We kept it platonic for a few months until one night I was out with a guy friend of mine at the movies, when we were leaving out; I bumped into Josh and one of his girlfriends. We introduced everybody and decided to go to get some food. We ended up a local pizza joint and made small talk. At the end of the night, I was at home about to go to bed when Josh showed up at my door.

"What are you doing here?" I asked.

"Is that old cornball dude you was with here?" he asked.

I laughed, he was in his feelings and I thought it was cute. "Since when do you care about who I kick it with?" I asked.

"I don't. At least I didn't before, until I saw you with that cornball ass dude, holding your hand and putting his arm around you. I didn't like it," he said.

I was taken back by his honesty, and I really didn't know what to say. I've told Josh plenty of times that I couldn't hang out with him because I had a date or plans, and he never tripped.

"You've never tripped before J, don't start tripping now."

Then he kissed me. At first, I backed off, but then he followed me and he kissed me again. That time, I let him. He held the back of my head, at the time I was rocking a short tapered cut like Rihanna, short in the back and along the sides, but long in the front. He had one hand on my head and the other on my ass, holding me close to him. When we broke our embrace, he asked, "Do you think you can be with a man like me?"

I wasn't sure what he was asking. "What do you mean?" I asked.

"I mean, no more dates, or plans with cornballs. Just me and you," he stated.

"Ok, I guess," I said

"I don't need you to guess, I need you to know. But before you decide, I need to show you something. Put some shoes on and come ride with me."

I did as I was told. That night he opened up his world to me. He took me to River Hills where is father lived. His father Hank; the largest, most prominent, heroin distributer in the Midwest, probably the U.S. Most people called him Mr. Milwaukee, because he owned everybody; the police, judges, the D.A., everyone was on his payroll. Last year when Brianna almost caught that case, he was the one to make the phone call that made everything go away.

I continued to explain to Brooke that Josh was next in line to take over his father's business. Even though Josh was a college graduate, owned a barbershop and went to law school part-time, his father expected him, and groomed him to take over one day. I told Brooke about the first time I did a drug run with Josh, when we drove to Flint to meet with one of his distributers. I explained how I would go with Josh every now and again to pick up money from the different drug houses they ran around the city.

I told her about this one time when I was with Josh. We met up with Bug and Jay, who both worked for his father, and one of their customers walked up on us looking for heroin. That same smell and look in their eyes that they had, Matt had the same thing. When I saw Matt that night, I talked to Josh about it. He called his dad. Come to find out Matt had been one of Bug's customers, and the word was put out that no one could serve him.

I looked at my sister and said, "When Matt walked me outside that night, I asked him if he was using heroin."

"You did? What did he say?" Brooke replied.

"He said that I was tripping."

"No wonder he was acting so different, his mood had completely changed, and he was actually nice that night. That explains a lot."

"So now do you believe me? I honestly did not know. And I damn sure wouldn't have kept it from you if I did."

"Yes, I'm sorry B. This is so fucked up. First Bri and now Matt; I don't know what I'm going to do." She began to cry again.

I held my sister while she cried; she was going through a lot. "What do you want to do B?" I asked, "You still wanna pack your stuff and leave?"

"Yes," she replied.

I waited for her to break our hug, and I followed my big sister upstairs to help her pack.

"Let's keep this incident to ourselves. Don't tell mom and dad, they have enough on their plate," she said.

I agreed. "And you just promise not to tell anyone about Josh."

"'I don't like it, but I won't. You just be careful when you're with him. That lifestyle may be fun and glamorous now, but it never ends pretty," she warned.

I thought about what my big sister said, and then quickly shook it off. We went upstairs and packed two suitcases then headed back home.

Harley

Mr. Williams and I made small talk after the ladies left. I told him a little about my construction company, my family, and myself. He shared some stories about Brianna and her sisters. We discussed current events, politics, and sports, anything that came up. As the day went on, I could tell he was getting tired, so I told him to relax on the recliner. We watched an episode of Martin and he was asleep before it went off. I couldn't sleep. I kept replaying the events of yesterday over and over in my head, trying to get a different outcome. However, none of that mattered. The reality of it all was lying helplessly in front of me.

My thoughts were interrupted by Brianna groaning and slightly moving her head. She caught me off guard; I quickly jumped to my feet and placed my hand on her head. "Gorgeous? Baby, can you hear me?" I said softly.

"Harley," she said, but she didn't open her eyes

I was a little choked up as I replied, "Yea baby, it's me."

She groaned a little more before she opened her eyes slightly. She smiled. I couldn't believe it, after all that she had been through, the pain she was still experiencing, and she still managed to smile. That smile broke me, and the tears I was fighting to hold back, escaped my eyes. I reached down and kissed her on her forehead before waking her father up.

"Mr. Williams, Mr. Williams, she's awake," I called out.

Brianna's father sprang to his feet and rushed to her side.

"Daddy!" she cried.

I watched as Brianna held on to her father and cried. She was so happy to see him, and he was thrilled to know his daughter was awake. I gave them a moment while I walked to the nurse's station to have someone come in and look her over. When I returned with the nurse, Brianna reached out for my hand. I held on to one and her father held on to the other as the nurse checked her monitors and asked her about her pain.

Brianna still seemed exhausted, so her father insisted that she get some rest. She made me promise not to leave her side, but I didn't have any plans to do that anyway. Her father called her mother to inform them that Brianna was awake, but she was still in need of some rest. I called my boy Jason to swing by and bring me a change of clothes; I also filled him in on what happened. I couldn't really discuss what I wanted to discuss, like how I planned to get at Kevin, because Brianna's dad was in the room, so I held off.

I was so happy to see her smile and to hear her voice. I said a silent prayer thanking God for pulling her through, and I remembered my promise to not touch Kevin, so I reluctantly let my grudge go. I was just happy to know that Brianna was going to pull through. I sat beside her bed until she fell back asleep. The nurse increased her pain medicine to help better manage her pain so she could rest. I held on to her hand, moved my chair closer to her bed, and laid my head next to hers. Within moments, I was also, fast asleep.

Chapter Nine

Brooke

I woke up to the sound of my mother's voice yelling, "She's awake, thank you Jesus, my baby is awake." I had fallen asleep in Bianca's room, and she was lying next to me knocked out. I shook her a few times to wake her up and tell her that Brianna was up and we needed to head to the hospital. We climbed out of bed and went to my parent's room.

"Come on girls. Let's get ready so you can take me back up to the hospital," she ordered

"Mom, what did daddy say? Is she talking? Is she in pain? How is she?" I asked.

"That's what we going to find out. Your daddy said she's resting right now, but she woke up a little while ago," she replied.

Bianca helped our mother get ready while I called and told Kris the good news. Since she didn't answer, I left a message, *"Hey Kris, you're probably still sleeping, I just wanted to let you know that Brianna is awake. We are heading over to the hospital now. Meet us there if you can. Love you, bye."*

I contemplated calling the hospital to check on Mathew. The medics said they were taking him to Froedert Hospital, the same hospital Brianna was at, but I wasn't ready to deal with that yet. I decided to hold off until after I knew that Bri was gonna be ok.

It didn't take us long before we were back at the hospital. When we walked into the room, Ryder was walking out the bathroom in a fresh set of clothes and my dad was sitting in the recliner; Brianna was asleep.

"I thought you said Bri was awake?" I asked my mom.

"She was for a while, but she was in pain so the doctors increased her pain medication so she could be comfortable," my dad said.

"Well, how did she seem to be doing?" my mom asked as she rubbed my sister's hair.

"She's strong Mrs. Williams. Even through the pain, she smiled and she's so happy that you two are here." Ryder said.

He looked to be in better spirits and that gave me some sort of comfort. I knew that if he believed that Bri was doing well after speaking to her, than she was going to be ok. We sat around for a few hours. Bianca and I made a run to get some food for everybody and it wasn't much longer after that, before Brianna started to stir in her sleep.

"Daddy?" she whispered.

"Yes, sweetheart, I'm here," Daddy said.

Bri opened her eyes and looked around the room. When she saw everyone, she smiled.

"Mommy!" she cried.

My mother got up, walked over to her and kissed her on her forehead. She sent for Bianca to get Brianna some water. "Here, drink this baby," Mom said.

Brianna did as she was told, and it must have helped because she was no longer whispering.

"How are you feeling Gorgeous?" Ryder asked as he sat in his same chair next to her bed.

Bri smiled and said, "You didn't leave."

"Of course not baby," he responded.

After they shared their moment, I went back to the original question that was asked.

"Bri, how are you feeling?"

"I'm ok I guess. I can't really feel anything," she said, and then she began to cry. I knew this would be hard for her. I couldn't imagine first of all being shot, but also being shot by someone you used to deeply love. Bianca and I joined our parents and Ryder around Bri's bed and tried to console her. She looked scared and exhausted. I hurt for my sister, we all did.

Brianna

I couldn't remember much from yesterday. I remember leaving the courtroom and getting into an argument with Kevin because he wanted me to leave with him. I remember Harley stepping in and telling Kevin to back off and it wasn't a good time. Then, there was a loud bang. I felt a burning sensation in my back and then everything went black. I remember hearing sirens and screams for a brief moment and the next thing I know, I'm waking up in a hospital room.

When I woke up, Harley was the first face I saw. He looked so stressed, he had dried blood on his shirt and he looked as though he needed some rest. He was probably worried sick. Then I saw Daddy, and I couldn't hold back my tears any longer. I was so happy to have my dad with me. With him around, I felt safe. I looked for my sisters and my mother, but they weren't there. I still had comfort in knowing that my dad and Harley stood by me, and that made me smile.

The nurse came in and asked me a few questions about my pain and how I felt. I felt like I had been hit by two trains and that I was a little lightheaded. She decided to increase my pain medication to help me rest. I started to ask her about my condition, but I was too tired to listen. When she walked out, the sound of the door slamming shut startled me. I held on tighter to Harley's hand and made him promise not to leave my side. The pain medication started working its magic and before I knew it, I was in a deep sleep; more like, consumed in a nightmare.

I dreamt that I was lying in the hospital bed asleep with my dad asleep in the recliner and Harley asleep in a chair next to my bed. All of a sudden, there was a loud commotion outside the door, followed by multiple gunshots. My father and Harley slept through the loud bangs and I tried to scream, but I had no voice. I tried to get up and wake up Harley and my dad, but I couldn't move. The gunshots stopped and on the other side of the door was silence. I remained still and listened. Suddenly, I heard footsteps and they became louder and louder as the person came closer to my room. I attempted to wake my dad and Harley, but still, I couldn't speak or move. I watched as the door handle turned and before it opened, I closed my eyes to pretend I was asleep.

I heard the intruder come inside the room. He was breathing heavily and each step he took sounded like thunder. I felt him stand over me and I felt him staring down at me. Next, I heard him walk away. I peeked a bit and saw that the intruder was Kevin. I noticed that he had walked over towards my dad. I began to panic, I saw him lift his gun. Still unable to move or speak, I tried my best to stop what was happening but I was helpless. Tears began to flow from my eyes as I watched him pull the trigger and kill my father. Three shots rang out, making Harley spring to his feet. Kevin turned around and shot at Harley. "BANG!" The bullet missed Harley and went through the wall above my bed. He let go another shot, this time pointed at me. Harley jumped on the bed in front of me as bullets were flying towards us; then, I woke up.

I was a bit panicked. I opened my eyes and that's when I saw my sisters and my mother. I was so scared; I didn't know what had happened to Kevin. I didn't know if he had been arrested or if he was out free to finish the job. I couldn't believe he actually shot me. My mother gave me some water and having her by my side and feeling her touch calmed me. Brooke was so concerned and when she asked me how I felt, I couldn't tell her that I was afraid or that my whole body ached. Therefore, I told her I was fine, that I couldn't feel anything. But the reality was that I was numb with fear.

I stayed up for a while and listened to my family make small talk and tell stories and jokes to keep the mood light. I couldn't help but to feel grateful for having such loving sisters, parents, and a strong man like Harley by my side. He continued to hold on to my hand and stay by my side, as if he was my life support. However, I appreciated him for that. I needed him more than he knew. He could have easily walked away from all of my drama, but he stuck by me. He was a good man.

It started getting late. My parents needed to get some rest, so Bianca offered to take them home. They kissed me and promised they would be back first thing in the morning. Harley stated he wasn't going to leave the hospital without me, and Brooke stayed a while to keep me company. My big sister looked so stressed.

"Brookie, are you ok?" I asked.

"Yea, I'm just worried about you B. I thought I was gonna lose you." She began to cry.

"Harley, do you mind getting Brooke something to drink?" I asked. I needed some alone time with my sister.

"Of course Gorgeous," he said and walked out the room.

Brooke walked over to my bed, sat in Harley's chair and laid her head next to mine. I loved my sister and I also knew her a lot better than she thought I did.

I asked, "B, what's on your mind? I know you're worried about me, but I'm fine. The doctor said that in a few days, the swelling may go down and then I can get out of bed and try walking. It will all work out. Don't cry."

She didn't respond, she just cried. I wrapped my arms around her as best I could. My mobility was very limited. We cried together, and I told her, "B, I'm scared."

"Scared of what?" she asked.

"Kevin. I keep having nightmares that he came to the hospital to kill me," I said.

"Kevin is in jail Bri. He's not getting out any time soon. He was arrested outside the courtroom. I think he was also shot by the officer," said Brooke.

This was news for me. I was happy to know that he was in police custody, but I still felt uneasy. Harley came back inside the room with two bottled waters and handed one to Brooke.

"Hey B, I'm gonna head home. I will be back first thing tomorrow morning ok?" said Brooke.

"Ok. Get some rest, and stop worrying. I'm fine," I said.

"How are you getting home?" Harley asked.

"I'm gonna take a cab."

"Put my number in your phone, text me and let us know you made it home safe."

Brooke took his number and kissed me and we said our goodbyes. When she left, Harley and I sat in silence for a while. I lay there, in the hospital bed with my eyes closed, slowly drifting back to sleep. Harley sat in his chair and held on to my hand with his head lying next to mine; then, he whispered, "I love you Brianna." I pretended not to hear him. Moments later, we were both asleep.

Brooke

I left my sister's room and walked to the front desk at the hospital.

"Excuse me, my name is Brooke Williams-Reed, I received a message that my husband, Matthew Reed was brought here," I stated.

I waited as the woman looked up Matt's information to provide me with his room number. Once I made it to his floor, I checked in at the nurse's station to talk to someone about his condition. The nurse that was taking care of Matthew filled me in on Matt's current condition. He was stable; they were going to keep him overnight for observation. Then, tomorrow, he would have the option to stay and attend their drug rehab program, or he could check himself out. She told me that when she did her rounds he was awake and watching television and I could go inside his room to see him if I liked.

I didn't know what I would say to Matthew. I was still dealing with the shock of finding him half dead on the floor due to a heroin overdose. I wasn't sure if I was ready to confront him or not. I stood outside his door, starring at it as if I could see through it. I thought about what the nurse said about the rehab program that Matthew would have a choice to attend, or he could choose to leave the hospital. I thought about the vows I took, *"For better, or for worse,"* and I decided to confront my husband.

I walked into the room and saw Matthew flipping through the channels on the small T.V. that hung in from the ceiling. When he saw me walk in, his eyes got as big as saucers, and he dropped the T.V. remote. I stood there in silence, looking at him. He was not the man that I married. The once beautiful blonde haired, blue-eyed man that stole my heart was no longer who I saw. The man I saw looked to be about twenty pounds lighter, his once golden blonde hair was now thin and dull looking, and those beautiful eyes that were once so full of life were now dim and no longer shined. He looked dead.

I stared at him and I wondered why I didn't see this before. I thought, *"How could I, have missed the signs."* Then I was reminded about the constant berating and the physical abuse forcing me to stay out of Matthew's way. I intentionally avoided him at all cost, afraid to stir up the anger inside him, not knowing what his triggers were. I continued to look at my dying husband.

"What's the matter Matthew? You weren't expecting me?" I asked.

Matthew looked down at his hands embarrassed to see me in his current state. He said, "I'm sorry."

I heard him, but it was as though he were speaking to himself. I asked, "What?"

"I said I'm sorry Brooke." He looked at me, "This was never supposed to happen. This isn't me."

"What exactly are you sorry for Matthew? Are you sorry that you have been beating the shit out of me damn near every day? Are you sorry for the mental abuse? Are you sorry for almost killing yourself today? ARE YOU SORRY FOR BEING A FUCKING HEROIN ADDICT?!!!" I screamed. Moments later two nurses came running inside.

"Mr. Reed is everything ok in here?" she asked.

"Yes, it's fine," he stated.

The nurse gave me a look as if to say, *shut the fuck up*, and said, "Ok, please let us know if you need anything." Then they left the room.

"Brooke, I'm sorry for everything, but..." he started to say more, but I cut him off.

"Matthew, I don't want to hear it. You have two choices, you stay here and go through rehabilitation, or you find someplace else to live, and I will file for divorce."

Matthew looked up at me, and his eyes were full of sadness and fear. I said, "I mean it Matthew. You need help."

"I know. I will go to rehab tomorrow," He said.

"Good, I will come by in the morning to bring you some clean clothes," I said.

"Thank you," he said.

I started to leave and before I walked out the door, Matthew called out. "Brooke." I turned to look at him and he said, "I love you and I'm sorry."

"Then, prove it Matthew," I said, and then continued out the door.

Kris

I couldn't believe what I just heard. As I sat holding my best friend as she broke down in my arms, I was still trying to process everything I was just told. Brooke had been beaten daily by her drug-addicted husband. It hurt my heart to know that my best friend, my sister, was carrying all of this pain alone. How did I not see that she was hurting? I wanted to kill Matthew! But he was already killing himself. I cried with my sister. So much turmoil was in our lives. Heartache and pain seemed to be all around us. I held on to Brooke and said a silent prayer for my family, the only real family I had. We sat and cried all night until we fell asleep on the sofa.

The next morning, I went home with Brooke to help her pack a bag for Matthew, today he started his drug rehab program. Brooke wanted to get to the hospital early because she didn't want to run into her family. The only other person that knew about Matthew's condition was Bianca. We hurried and grabbed a few things then headed to the hospital. Brooke wanted some time alone, so she drove her car and I followed behind.

In route to the hospital, I received a phone call from a blocked number. I figured it could be Brianna calling from the hospital since I overslept and didn't get a chance to see her yesterday. I answered the phone, "Hello?"

"Um hello…" they responded.

It didn't take long for me to figure out who it was, and her voice nearly caused me to rear end Brooke. I wondered if she would call, or if I should call her. I wondered how I would react when I talked to her or saw her. Silence; I didn't know what to say. I waited, the light turned green and I continued to follow Brooke. When I realized she wasn't going to speak I said, "What do you want? You're not dead, so I guess you didn't oblige my request."

"I tried, but the pills didn't work. I panicked," she responded.

I thought she was joking, but she didn't laugh. I remained silent, speechless.

"Krystal, I wanted to apologize for everything. You didn't deserve what I did to you. I'm really sorry and I'd like a chance to tell you that face to face," she said.

"You can't be serious. Save that shit for somebody else, you're the reason my sister was shot! Fuck you bitch; I should've killed you myself." I started to hang up but I heard her say, "Shot! Who was shot?" she sounded surprised.

"Oh, you don't know? Your boyfriend shot Brianna." And with that, I hung up the phone.

As we pulled into the parking structure of the hospital, I laughed. Maybe it was to release some nervous energy, or pinned up frustration, but I laughed uncontrollably, and eventually I let out a loud scream. I was hurt; I was angry; I was confused. I couldn't believe Dee tried to kill herself. I wondered how I would've felt, had she succeeded. I immediately erased that thought. I turned off the engine on my car and got out to meet Brooke at the elevator.

"You ready to do this?" I asked Brooke.

"Yea," she said and we took the elevator up to the 12th floor were Matthew was.

As we walked to the room, one of the nurses stopped us.

"Excuse me, you're here to see Mr. Reed right?" she asked Brooke.

"Yes, I came to bring him some clean clothes to take with him," Brooke responded

"I'm sorry, but the Social Worker and the Program Manager already came by to pick him up. If you like, you can leave the bag with me, and when they get back, I can hand it over to the Social Worker."

"No, that won't be necessary; I can take it to him. Do you have the address to the facility?" Brooke asked.

"Yes, the facility is called Better Days, but they can't have visitors for the first sixty days. Let me take your contact information and I will have the Program Manager give you a call," she said.

Brooke reluctantly wrote down her contact information and gave that and the bag of Matthew's belongings to the nurse, and then we headed downstairs to visit with Brianna. On the way down, I asked Brooke if she was ok. She said she was fine, but I could tell that she was disappointed. I didn't press her about it anymore; I knew she needed some time.

When we walked into Bri's room, she and Harley was still sleeping. We didn't want to wake them, so we went downstairs to the cafeteria to get coffee and see if they had anything good for breakfast. When we walked into the busy cafeteria, full of first and third shift doctors and nurses getting their morning fix of coffee and breakfast, the morning news caught my attention.

"Brooke, you see this?" I said.

They were highlighting the story of Bri's shooting outside of the courtroom. The headline read, 'Local Milwaukee Nightclub Owner Arrested for Shooting'. They mentioned that Kevin was shot in the shoulder, but was fine and was released into police custody. They mentioned that they did not know the extent of Brianna's injuries, but that she was in the hospital in critical condition from their last update. They were speculating as to what could have caused Kevin to start shooting. All they knew was that he had no history of arrests, or mental illness. They were still trying to find out if the shooting was planned and if the victim, Brianna, was targeted.

I shook my head, "That's crazy."

"I hope they put his ass under the jail," Brooke said.

We grabbed our coffee and a bagel. Brooke grabbed an extra coffee for Harley, and we headed up to spend the rest of the day with Bri.

Chapter Ten

Kevin

After refusing to speak with the detectives and waiting over six hours to be processed at the county jail, I was finally able to make my phone call. I wanted to call up to the hospital to check on Bri, but I knew that wouldn't be a smart move. I felt like shit for what I did, I never meant to hurt her. She was supposed to be my wife, I never had any intention of hurting her; it was that dread headed dude that I wanted to hurt. I let my pride get the best of me and now, I was at a point of no return. I had no one in my corner, and as I dialed the numbers to make my phone call, I prayed that I hadn't completely burned this bridge either.

The phone rang a few times before she answered, "Deanna Phillips."

"What's up Dee, it's me. I need your help."

"What is all of this I'm hearing about you allegedly shooting Brianna?" she asked.

"That's why I need your help I'm at the county and I need a lawyer. Can you help me? You know I'm good for it," I asked.

"I will send a friend of mine to help you because I love you and I know deep down you're a good person, but don't ever call me again." And with that, she hung up in my face. I was all alone. I felt like shit, but I deserved it. As soon as I placed the phone back on the hook, as if on cue, the guard came over and escorted me to my cell.

It wasn't like in the movies, like when you walk down the halls where you're surrounded by hundreds of other inmates and it's loud and busy.

No, it was quiet, dark, and dank. I was placed in a cell all alone, surrounded by cold and dirty walls. I had no one to talk to. No one to come over to me and ask me, "What you in for?" The last thing I needed right now was to be alone, with my thoughts.

I tried to convince myself that everything was going to be ok. I had never been to jail or in any kind of legal trouble. I didn't know what to expect. I didn't know what kinds of questions to ask my attorney, I didn't know if I should've just answered the detective's questions and let the D.A. work a deal out for me. I was terrified. On top of all of that, I still didn't know how Brianna was doing. All of the worrying consumed me and I began to panic.

I felt like the walls were closing in on me. I began to have trouble breathing, my heart was racing, and I began to sweat. My vision started to blur and the tiny cell seemed to be spinning in circles. I clutched the cold steel bedframe as I tried to calm myself and regain my composure. I leaned my back against the cold concrete wall, closed my eyes, and wished that it were all just a bad nightmare.

A few hours later, a guard came by and escorted me to a private visiting room to meet with my attorney. I walked into the room and a middle aged, short, white man with a no nonsense glare on his face greeted me.

"Kevin James, I am Joseph Kahn. I am here on behalf of Philips and Associates," he spoke, introducing himself.

"Nice to meet you Mr. Kahn. Do you have a list of my charges? You think you can help me?" I asked.

"Well first, I need you to explain to me what happened. You have some pretty serious charges here. Attempted Murder, Discharging a Firearm in Public, and Endangering Public Safety. You could be looking at over twenty years easy. My job is to get you the minimal sentence possible."

"Twenty years? I can't do Twenty years! I'm not a criminal, I made one stupid mistake," I exclaimed.

"Calm down Mr. James. I assure you I will do the best I can. You have a lot going for yourself. One, the victim is expected to make a full recovery, two, you have never been in trouble, three, the gun was registered in your name and four, you are a pillar of the community. I am fairly certain that I can get the judge to grant bail, while we work out your defense," he said confidently.

That sounded good to me. We arranged to meet tomorrow morning when I appeared in court for arraignment. In the meantime, I guess I was stuck in this hellhole for the night, hoping I could be home in my own bed tomorrow. As they escorted me back to my cell, I thought about what he said about Brianna, she was expected to make a full recovery. I was happy to know that she was going to be ok. I thought to myself, maybe when this was all over, she would give me a chance to make things up to her.

As I entered my cell for the second time, I felt a little more at peace. I would be going home tomorrow, Brianna was gonna pull through, so I had no worries. I knew that I was looking at some time for what I did, but I was confident that my lawyer would get me a plea agreement so I wouldn't have to do twenty years. I lay back on the thin mattress and tried to figure out a plan on how I could get Brianna to forgive me.

I sat outside the courtroom, hands and feet cuffed, waiting to be called inside. My lawyer was nowhere to be found. I started getting anxious and nervous. They sat us along the bench in the order we were going to be called in; I had one guy in front of me. I continued to look around and scan the hall for my attorney. As I looked around, I saw two familiar faces, Bianca and her mother, Mrs. Williams. There were two guys following behind them, one of them was Bianca's boyfriend, the other I didn't know. I hurriedly looked away; I couldn't face them right now.

My heart sank, it couldn't be a good sign that they were there. They probably came to ensure that I stayed locked up. I got angry. *Where the fuck is my lawyer?* I thought. The guy in front of me was called in, and I began to go into full panic mode. I asked the guard if I could make a call, but he dismissed my request. I sat, nervously shaking my right leg as I continued to scan the halls. Moments later, my lawyer came around the corner walking briskly to where I was sitting.

"Man, where the fuck you been?" I yelled.

"Sorry, Mr. James. May I have a moment with my client please?" he asked the guard.

The guard allowed me to sit at the bench across from everyone to discuss proceedings with my lawyer. "So, what's the plan?" I asked.

"Well, the D.A. will present the charges against you; the judge will ask you for a plea, you will plead not guilty, and then the judge will ask for a recommendation on bail. The D.A. will request remand, at which point I will point out that you do not have any priors, you're not a flight risk and you have a business to run. The judge will make a decision to either send you to the secure detention facility until trial or send you home," he explained.

I started to ask him what my odds were, but at that moment, I was called in to see the judge. Everything went down exactly how my lawyer said it would, the only difference was, when he brought up the fact that I had no priors and highlighted my contributions to the community, the slick ass D.A. pointed out that I opened fire outside a crowded courthouse and made me out to be a menace. The judge didn't need much convincing, and demanded that I be held without bail. That was it, my ass was being sent to lock up.

Chapter Eleven

Brianna

It's been four months since I was released from the hospital. Most of the physical pain was gone, but I still had some tenderness around the area where they had to cut me open to retrieve the bullet that was lodged in my large intestine. I had a huge scar on my stomach that went all the way around to my back. I had scarring from the staples they used to close me back up, and I had a huge scar on the other side of my back where the other bullet went through and damaged my kidney. Each day I stood in the mirror looking at the scars crying and regretting the day that I ever met Kevin.

Today was no different; as I stood in the mirror looking at my wounds, tears began to fall. I ran my hands across my stomach and lightly touched the thick snake like scar. I felt so ugly and ruined. I could never wear a bikini again, I could never wear my favorite dress with the low-cut exposed back, there was so much that Kevin took away from me. I didn't feel confident anymore. I didn't feel desirable. And every day, I felt scared.

As I looked in the mirror, I had flashbacks of all that happened and I kept wondering why me. Asking God, what did I do so wrong that this had to happen to me? I hadn't left the house since I left the hospital, too afraid of what would happen to me. Loud noises gave me anxiety, I had trouble sleeping, and I was sure that I was pushing Harley away. I could hear Harley's voice in my head saying, *"Gorgeous, you are still and always will be, the most beautiful woman in the world to me."* I knew he was genuine, but I couldn't see it. He told me this every night, he hasn't left my side since I left the hospital. But I still continued to sleep with my back turned to him, fully dressed, too ashamed to allow him to seem me scarred like this; and I wondered, how long will he stay.

Before my mom and dad left, my mother told me that I was beautiful and she could see that I was hurting and how I was treating Harley. She told me, "You can have your moment right now. You can cry and feel sorry for yourself. However, when you're done, thank God for keeping you, and don't turn bitter. You have a good man in Harley, be good to him." I remembered those words, and I knew she was right. I called out to Harley, "Harley, baby can you please come in here with me?"

I continued to stand there, crying silently, when Harley walked into the bathroom, he was shocked to see me standing there, naked. He came to me and began wiping away my tears. He kissed my forehead and asked, "What can I do, to make it better?" I held on to him, and he held me close. I told him, "I'm sorry for pushing you away."

"I'm not going anywhere, baby I told you that. I understand it's hard, but you will get through this. We will get through this together. Ok?" he said and he kissed me again.

I kissed him back. He placed his hand behind my head and brought me closer to him. It felt so good to be in his arms again and embraced in his kiss. I let go of all of my worries at that moment and enjoyed my man. I asked him to join me in the shower. I stepped in first while he got undressed.

He washed my body gently and I washed his. When we were done, he wrapped me in a large soft towel.

When we got back to the room, he rubbed my body with coconut oil. When he reached the scar on my stomach, I flinched, wanting to hide and cover up, but he held onto me, kneeled down, and trailed kisses along my hideous scar. I began to cry, he was so good to me. He continued to rub oil down my body and then he told me to turn over. I turned onto my stomach as he rubbed my back with oil and placed soft kisses on the scars on my back. He continued to oil the rest of my body. When he was finished, he climbed in bed next to me; his towel still wrapped around his waist.

I got up and laid my head on his chest, and he began to wrap his arms around me and stroke my locs. "I love you so much," I said.

"I love you more," he said.

I lifted my head and kissed him, he pulled me up until I was completely on top of him. We kissed and held each other. I reached down to remove his towel, he stopped, "Are you sure you're ready to do this?" he asked.

"Yes, baby I'm sure." I said, and then removed the towel from around his waist. I could feel the girth and strength of his manhood pressed against me. I kissed him again as he turned me over onto my back. He broke our embrace and lifted himself up on his hands, he looked me in my eyes, and his long locs fell on either side of my head, surrounding me. I looked into his eyes, and he said, "You're so beautiful." He leaned down, careful not to put his whole weight on me, and he trailed kisses from my forehead, to my nose, then to my lips. Then he kissed my collarbone and licked me from my collarbone, up my neck, and back down. His touch was so gentle and strategic and my body was on fire.

Harley then trailed kisses to my breasts, each one he paid close attention to, lightly biting and sucking one, while he caressed the other. His kisses trailed lower and once again, he was kissing my scar. He whispered, "You're so beautiful." I closed my eyes and let my head fall back into my pillow. His touch felt amazing to me as I kept hearing him say over and over in my head, "You're so beautiful." His kisses trailed lower and lower, until he reached my hot spot.

By this time, my body was inflamed. I was so wet; my juices began to spill over onto the sheets. Harley took his finger and ran it between my lower lips, he dipped it inside of me, and I let out a soft moan. I opened my eyes to look at him as he sucked my fluids off his finger. He saw me looking, and he dipped his finger inside me again, but this time, he took it out and placed it on my lips, and I sucked my juices off him. Before I knew it, Harley's face was between my legs, bringing me to my first orgasm of the night.

My legs were spread wide, feet planted on the bed, knees bent; my back arched as far as it would go, I was riding the wave as Harley continued to lick and suck me into euphoria. I had to grab him by his locs and pull him up for air; my clit was too sensitive to allow him to continue. He kissed me and once again, I tasted my own release. I craved him, and I begged to return the favor, but he wouldn't allow me to. Instead, he rose up and continued to kiss me as he filled me up.

I felt my walls stretch to let him in; I lost my breath for a minute as he entered me. I felt whole again. As he slow stroked me, I held on with my arms around his neck, moaning in ecstasy. He went deeper, his hands griping my ass, pulling me into him. I let out a slight groan.

"Aaaah." He had pressed a little too hard on the scar on my back.

"I'm sorry baby. Do you want me to stop?" he asked.

"No, please don't stop."

He continued to carefully stroke me, deeper and deeper. I rolled my hips to match his rhythm as he moaned in my ear. Then he said, "Turn over for me."

I did as I was instructed, and was now on all fours. Harley moved me to the edge of the bed and stood behind me. He rubbed and kissed my back and bit me on my ass. Then, he slowly entered me from behind. He stroked long and hard, as he held on to my waist. I had to bury my face in a pillow to muffle my screams of ecstasy. I bit my pillow and held on tight to my sheets as Harley slow stroked me to heaven. We came together, just like our first time, and then, I fell fast asleep in his arms.

Brooke

I pulled up to Better Days Rehabilitation Center over thirty minutes ago, but I couldn't find the strength to go in. I spoke to the Program Manager about a month and a half ago, and he told me the same thing the nurse told me, that they didn't allow visitation or any outside contact for the first sixty days of the program. Today was the day that he could finally have visitors and I was too scared to go inside to see him. I called my best friend for a pep talk, before I convinced myself to drive away.

"Hello?" she answered.

"Kris, I can't do it. I'm out here and I can't find the courage to go inside."

"Brooke, just calm down. It's natural to be nervous. Do you want me to come up there? I can leave work right now."

"No, don't do that. I just needed a pep talk that's all."

"Well, get your ass in there and see your husband. He's sixty-plus days clean, he probably looking fine as hell again. Did you bring a fresh pair of panties with you?" She laughed.

I was glad I called her; she always knew how to lighten the mood. She was right; Matthew was clean for more than sixty days now. I hope that he was back to the old him, or close to it. Then I realized, it has been more than sixty days, and I hadn't received a phone call from him. I stopped laughing and got serious again.

"He didn't call," I said.

"What did you say? I didn't hear you," responded Kris.

"Matthew, he didn't call me. He could make phone calls and get visitors after sixty days and he didn't call me. He doesn't even know I'm coming," I said.

"Well maybe he didn't know what to say B. But you won't know that sitting outside," she fussed.

"Yea, you right. Let me get in here, and I will call you back."

"Ok, love you girl."

"Love you too, bye."

I looked in the mirror and checked my hair and makeup, then headed inside to see my husband. Once I got inside, I stood in line at the check in desk. The waiting room was a bit crowded with families of the men and women in the program, some of them even brought small children with them. I looked around at everyone waiting patiently to be called back to the visiting area. It was finally my turn to check in.

"Hi, I'm here to see Matthew Reed."

"Reed." The woman said; as she checked the computer, I waited. "I'm sorry, but I'm showing that Matthew Reed checked out and is no longer in the program."

"Checked out? How could he check out?" I asked.

"Well it's a voluntary program, unless ordered by the court, the participants can check out whenever they like, "said the woman at the desk.

"And no one called to inform me?" I was furious.

"I'm sorry ma'am, but unless the participant is a minor. We aren't obligated to inform family members or spouses of any changes in the program or if someone checks out," she stated.

"Well, can you at least tell me when he checked out? I'm his wife; the least you can do is tell me that."

The woman looked back at her computer, punched a few keys and said, "About a month ago, I'm very sorry Mrs. Reed."

I walked out stunned. I couldn't believe that Matthew checked out of the facility a month ago and hasn't come home, called, or nothing. Where was my husband? I tried calling him on his cell; however, it went straight to voicemail. I called his job, spoke to his manager and was told that Matthew had been fired more than three months ago. I started to panic, and once I was inside my car, I completely broke down. I was scared for my husband; I didn't know if he was ok, if he was somewhere dead from an overdose, I didn't know what to think. And I was angry. I felt abandoned and betrayed. I cried and screamed in my car, until I couldn't cry anymore. I called my sister,

Bianca answered, "What's up B, how did it go?"

"It didn't, he fucking checked out," I said.

"What? Damn, when?" she asked.

"Over a month ago B. He hasn't called, tried to come home, nothing. Where's my husband Bianca?" I cried.

"Don't cry B. Why don't you come over and I can make some phone calls?" she said.

I took a moment to gain my composure and headed to the house to see Bianca. I prayed that she could find out where my husband was and if he was ok. I drove in silence so that I could sort out my thoughts. A few blocks from the house, I got a call from Kris, I updated her on what happened, and she told me she would meet me at the house when she got off work.

When I arrived, Bianca, Brianna, Harley and Josh were sitting around the kitchen talking. Bianca caught Brianna up on everything that was going on. Josh had made some calls to his friends to see if any of them had seen Matthew. While we waited for a response, I listened to everyone else's random conversations. Kris came in shortly after and we chatted for a bit. She made me laugh and tried to take my mind off everything that was going on.

When the word came back from Josh's friends that Matthew hasn't been around, I left and went home. I wanted to be there in case my husband decided to show up.

Kris

"Kris, just hear me out I have something important to tell you about Kevin's case," said Dee.

I couldn't believe this bitch was still calling me. I was getting calls all throughout the day and night from blocked numbers. I knew it was her calling, so I refused to answer. Today, I was just fed up and wanted the calls to stop.

"What!" I yelled.

"The attorney contacted me and said that they were entering a plea deal with the D.A., the charge would go down to the one charge of aggravated assault with a deadly weapon and a sentence of ten years. He could end up doing the whole ten years, or it could be split with time served in prison and time on probation, but that would be up to the judge."

"Ten years? That's it?" I asked. I couldn't believe what I was hearing. "He could have killed her," I said.

"I know. You should have Brianna go to the plea hearing and make a statement. That will encourage the judge to give him more time locked up," she suggested.

"Why are you helping us, when this is your fault?" I asked.

She paused then said, "I know I was out of line for what I did, and I can accept that. But it takes two, number one, and number two, Kevin is his own man. He made the decision to pull that trigger; I was not there holding his hand making him do it."

"Yea, well, you see it your way, and I see it mine." I started to hang up.

"Wait," she said.

"Yea?"

"One more thing, Kevin signed some paperwork, giving the club to Brianna as restitution for her injuries. I need her to come to my office and sign the paperwork," she went on to explain.

"You sure that's a good idea?" I asked.

"I know. I offered to go over the paperwork with her when Kevin's lawyer brought it up. I figured it would be a good time for me to apologize for everything. Plus, I have her meeting me at the office so she wouldn't kill me," she said half-jokingly. She was aware of what went down with Maria the trainer.

"Wow, ok I will let her know," I said, and then hung up.

I called Brooke to check on her, she didn't sound too well. She said that Matthew had been home, because the car was gone when she got there. She sounded like she was crying, so I decided to stop by and keep her company. On the way over, I stopped at the gas station not too far from where she lived. I went inside to grab bottled water, and as I stood at the pump filling my tank, I saw Matthew pull into the gas station. He looked terrible. His hair was untamed, his clothes were dirty, and his skin looked pale, almost gray. I watched him as he walked into the store. I didn't want him to see me, so I hurried and finished pumping my gas, and got in the car.

When he came out, he sat in the car for a while and opened his fresh pack of cigarettes. He lit the cigarette and started the car; I followed him. As I watched him, I called Brooke.

"Hello?" she answered.

"B, I just saw Matthew at the gas station and I'm following him now."

"What? What do you mean you're following him, where are you?" she asked.

"I was at the gas station off of 27th Street, but we are headed south. I'm gonna follow him and see where he's going," I said.

"I'm on my way!"

"No wait; we don't know where he's going. I will call you when he stops."

"OK. Make sure you do," she said, and then she hung up the phone.

I followed Matthew, making sure not to follow too close. We drove for about thirty minutes until we made it to a small suburb of Milwaukee. He got out of the car and walked around to the back of an old house. I looked around to see if anyone was outside. I waited a while, then got out of my car and followed him around back. By the time I made it to the back door, he was already inside. I heard music coming from inside, and I looked down through the basement window, and I could see about four or five people sitting on the floor of the basement, it looked like they were sleeping. One of the guys was tying a string around his arm, prepping to receive his fix.

I ran back to my car and drove off. I called Brooke immediately. "I know where Matthew has been staying," I said.

Chapter Twelve

Brianna

Harley and I waited in the reception area, but we didn't have to wait for long before Dee strutted out to the lobby. I had to admit, she was a beautiful woman. She lacked morals, but she was beautiful. She always exuded sex. In the past, I wasn't worried because I always thought that she played for the other team. I guess that was all a part of Kevin's plan too, to make me believe his side chick was just a lesbian friend and business partner, and not a bisexual hoe. But that was then, and I was over it all. I had a man who loved me flaws, scars and all. Harley helped me to build up my confidence to come out the house.

He convinced me to face Kevin at the hearing and to tell the judge how I was affected by the event. I also had a chance to look him in the eye and I'm sure he could see the rage that I tried so hard to keep hidden. The judge ended up giving him ten years, eight in prison with the chance of early release with good behavior. He had to do a minimum of five years and any time not done in prison would be paroled. Did I think it was enough time? No, but I was ready to move forward with my life. There was still some uneasiness that I felt when we left the courtroom. I felt the need to make Kevin pay for what he did to me. I didn't know how, or when, but he was going to pay.

We were at Dee's office finishing up the last pieces of this mess. Last month, Kevin had given me his most prized possession, his nightclub. At first, I wasn't going to take it. However, after talking it over with my sisters and my fiancé, yes Harley proposed, I decided to take the club, quit my job, and discover a new business venture. We followed her to the meeting room. She explained each of the documents that I had to sign to take possession of the club. When we were finished, she asked Harley if she could speak with me alone. Harley reluctantly obliged and stepped out into the hallway.

"Brianna, I know things have been rough for you and I know that I'm a huge part of that. I wanted to apologize for what I've done. It was very selfish of me and foolish. I wish I could take it back," she said.

"I don't," I said. "If you and Kevin hadn't done what you did, I would have never met Harley. So, I forgive you for what you did to me and my sister. However, you need to know that you really missed out. Kris is a wonderful, loving person, and you will not find anyone else like her. Oh and tell Kevin, to watch his back, this ain't over."

With that, I smiled, thanked her for her services, walked out to join my fiancé in the hall, and we were on our way to my new property. Harley and I had plans to renovate the space and turn it into luxury condominiums right in the heart of downtown Milwaukee. Things were really starting to look up for me. I knew once Dee relayed the message, Kevin would be looking over his shoulder for the next five to eight years. I knew that Kevin would feel the same fear that I felt for three whole months before facing him in court, and that gave me the peace I needed to move on.

Months later, I received letter after letter from Kevin begging for forgiveness and telling me how much he loved me. Harley was fed up and paid him a visit, after that the letters stopped. I'm not sure what he did or said to Kevin, but he was no longer an issue. After that, we moved my things out of my parent's house and into our own home, and we never spoke of Kevin again.

Brooke

I had been watching this house almost every night since Kris told me about it. I've seen Matthew enter and exit more times than I can count. A week ago, I had to have a locksmith come out to the house to change the locks because Matthew came home while I was at work and stole my T.V. and stereo system out of the front room. I was fed up, and tonight, I planned to confront him.

I turned off my headlights and got out of my vehicle. I walked up to the house and around back to the back door. I didn't have to knock because it was wide open. I walked up the stairs first, to where I heard voices. I peeked around the corner and saw three white guys in the kitchen cooking what I could only assume was drugs. I backed away from the door and proceeded down the basement stairs.

Once down there, I found Matthew nodding off in a back corner. I walked over to him and shook him a bit to wake him up. He looked up at me, "Brooke?" Then nodded off again.

"Matthew, come on let's go," I said.

"Go home Brooke," he said.

"No, I'm not leaving you here. Come on, let's get you some help Matthew." I began to cry.

"Look, I said go home you black dirty bitch. LEAVE!" he yelled, and then he pushed me.

"But Matthew…" before I could continue, Matthew crawled over to me and began to choke me.

"Get the fuck out of here you dumb nigger bitch," he said.

225

I was so hurt, and I could barely breathe with him choking me. I broke away and ran up the stairs and out of the house. When I made it to my car, I sat there and cried for a while. I was so hurt and angry. I pulled out the gun I brought with me every night that I sat outside this house. I took the safety off the gun and waited until Matthew came back outside. It felt like I was waiting for hours, and I was just about to leave when I saw Matthew coming out, stumbling to his car. I started up my car, and drove up beside him real close. I rolled the window down, stuck my arm out the window, gun in my hand, and fired three shots directly into his chest. I watched him fall to the ground, and then I sped off.

There was no adrenaline rush, no sense of panic, or regret after what was done. I felt justified. It had to be done. I continued on my route home, stopping to throw the gun in the lake along the way. I didn't call my sisters and I didn't call Kris. I didn't tell anyone what I did. When I got home, I showered and had the best night sleep I've had in a very long time.

The next day, the shooting was on the news. They didn't release the name or any information on the victim, but I knew it was Matthew. At the time, the police had no suspects. They did however, bust the drug house, and the killing is suspected to be connected to a drug transaction gone bad. I smiled and turned the T.V. off.

Later that day, I had two detectives at my door informing me that my husband was shot and killed. They asked me a bunch of questions about

Matthew's drug habits and where he hung out, who he hung out with, blah, blah, blah. I played the caring, worried, sad wife role. Then I had to follow them to the coroner's office to identify the body. I called my sisters so they could be there for support.

My sisters met me at the coroner's office. I looked at Matthew one last time and I left him lying there on the cold slab. I expected to feel sad, or disappointment, but I was relieved. As we walked out of the coroner office, I held each of my sisters' hands and in my hand as I started making funeral arrangements. To my sisters, I was being the strong big sister. They had no idea that I finally felt free.

My sisters were very helpful and supportive. I decided to have Matthew cremated, and decided that I would not have a funeral, but I would hold a memorial for him. I called and told my parents what happened and they made plans to fly out for the memorial. I called Matthew's parents, but they had known of his drug addiction as well and didn't want anything to do with him. He didn't have any siblings, so it was up to me to make all of the decisions.

The following week was the memorial for Matthew. Everything seemed so final then, and I found myself feeling overwhelmed for a moment. As we walked hand in hand down the isle of the small church, I looked around shocked by the amount of people who came out. Some were relatives who looked vaguely familiar, but most were members of the church who came to show their support. Everyone was whispering their condolences, and bowing their heads as we made our way through. I tried to focus my attention straight ahead, avoiding eye contact with anyone. I focused my attention on the flower arrangements. The white lilies had a sort of calming effect and helped to put my mind at ease. That is until I glanced over at the life size portrait mounted next to the coffin. My knees slightly buckled and I felt my sisters' grips tighten as they lead the way to our seats.

We took our places upfront, and shortly after, the presiding pastor opened with prayer. We all closed our eyes and bowed our heads, most of the people in the church quietly touching and agreeing with the pastor's words, me, saying a separate prayer to save my soul for what I did. As I replayed the last moments in my mind, tears began to stream down my eyes. It wasn't remorse for what I did, but a release of finally being free from the pain. A sign of relief from all of the pinned up emotions I kept hidden from everyone. Silent tears, escalating to loud, heart wrenching cries. My life would never be the same. Everyone started looking my way, concerned; believing that my heart was aching unbearably, but inside, I was elated.

It had been a rough year so far. Brianna's broken engagement, being shot, getting engaged again, and starting a new business. Bianca's in love with the son of a heroin dealer. Kris finding out she was a lesbian. And with me, killing my racist, drug addicted abuser of a husband. I was so ready to end this year, and looking forward to the joys that 2016 was going to bring.

After the memorial service, my parents went on home, and my sisters and I stayed behind to thank the guest for coming. Most of the people in the church were gone and as the last group was leaving Bianca, Bri, and Kris went outside to give me some time alone with Matthew's remains. His parents, although they did not come to the memorial service, insisted that they possess Matthew's ashes; I didn't put up a fight. He was better off with them anyway. His father wasn't too happy with his mother's decision, but he relented. They were coming by later to get him.

As I stood silently, saying my last goodbyes, I felt someone standing behind me. I turned around, and a woman that I never saw before was staring at me. She looked lost. He clothes were stained, her hair was matted, and she smelled as though she hadn't showered in days.

"Can I help you?" I asked.

"No, I'm just here to see a friend," she responded, as she walked up to Matthew's urn.

"You knew my husband?"

"Yes. And I know you too," she stated, still looking at the urn.

"I'm not sure we ever met. What's your name?" I asked.

"You killed him!" she yelled.

I looked around and no one else was in the church. "Come again?" I said.

"I saw you, you shot him," she said.

I was stunned. I didn't think to worry about if anyone had seen me. "You must be mistaken, I…" I started to deny it, when she cut me off.

"No, I know it was you, I was standing right there. I was there in the basement when you came to get him and he choked you. I was there. You killed him!"

At that moment, I started to panic. Bianca walked back in the church looking around, most likely looking for me. I began to yell, "Get out! How dare you bring that filth to my husband's memorial! Get out!"

"What's going on?" Bianca came rushing over.

"She's Matthew's drug buddy and I want her out of here! How dare you come in here high and causing a scene?" I yelled at her.

The woman walked towards the door, before she left out, she turned and said, "You won't get away with this." Then left out the church.

"What was that all about B? Are you ok?" Bianca asked

"Yea, I'm fine, let's just go." I said

As we walked out of the church, I was thinking how I was going to solve this new problem I had. No one would believe a drug addict over me, but somehow, I had to find her and make sure she didn't talk. I found myself back at the house where it all began. I sat outside trying to convince myself to go home, but something in me couldn't do it. I sat, and I waited for the girl to show up, but she never did. After a few hours, I gave up and headed home.

On the way home, I got a call from Bianca.

"B, I'm at your house. I know where you at, leave now and meet me here," she said.

"What do you mean you know where I'm at…hello?" Bianca had already hung up the phone.

When I got home, Bianca, Josh, and the two guys she brought to the house when Matthew overdosed, were sitting at my kitchen table.

"What's going on here?" I asked nervously.

"B, I know what happened. I know what you did, and we took care of that problem for you," Bianca said calmly.

"Problem? What problem?" I asked.

"B, I heard everything the fiend said to you at the church. It all made sense, I know you shot and killed Matt, but did you have to be so damn sloppy?" she asked.

"I wasn't thinking. I just remember him choking me, calling me a nigger, and I lost it." I began to cry, remembering our last encounter. I still loved Matthew, but I wasn't sorry for what I did.

"It's ok B. I had Bugs track down ole girl, and it's taken care of no worries. Next time, just come to me first," she said as she held me.

I was so surprised at how calm she was, and when she said they took care of it, I knew what she meant. I wondered when my baby sister became so cold and calculated. I knew she was only looking out for me, but the way she said it, it sounded as if she'd done this before. I didn't question it. I just thanked them for looking out for me, and retreated upstairs to my bedroom to get some rest. Bianca, Josh, and their muscle let themselves out.

Bianca

After leaving Brooke's place, I wasn't feeling well. I went home and felt sick to my stomach. I couldn't remember my last period and I started to panic. I took five tests and they all came to the same conclusion, but I couldn't accept it. Now, instead of hanging out with my sisters at the house, drinking, and eating, I'm here at the clinic laying on a cold table waiting to get an ultrasound. As I lay waiting, I was trying again to remember when the last time I had a period. With everything going on, I had completely lost track. I waited impatiently for the doctor to come back.

A few moments later, in walked the doctor with a huge grin on her face, "Hello Ms. Williams, are you ready for your ultrasound?" she asked.

"Yea, sure," I responded unenthusiastically.

She lifted my gown and placed the cold gel on my belly. After moving the magic wand around my belly for a few moments, there it was. A little black dot.

"Congratulations Ms. Williams. I would say you're about seven weeks pregnant."

"What, that's it? Don't you have to draw blood or something to confirm?" I asked. I was so confused and scared too. *What would my sisters think? What would Josh say?* So many thoughts ran through my mind as I laid on the cold table staring at the computer screen.

"I will get this printed for you, and I will write you a prescription for prenatal vitamins. You can go ahead and get dressed," she said as she walked out of the room.

I put my shirt back on and sent a text to Josh to meet me at the house. I figured I might as well get everyone together and tell them at the same time. When the doctor came back in, she gave me the ultrasound photo and the prescription and I was on my way. I didn't know whether to cry or to be happy about this. There was no way I was ready to be a mother, but now, I didn't have a choice.

I drove home in silence. Josh still hadn't responded to my text, so when I got home, I sat in the car and called him. His phone rang once, and then went to voicemail. I left him a message, and got out the car to join my sisters. It's been two days since Matthew's memorial and Brooke wanted us to spend some sister time together. When I walked in, they were already in the living room, laughing, drinking wine, and playing Twister.

"It's about time you showed up, we need a spinner. Hurry up and pour you a drink so you can help us out," said Brooke.

"I'm pregnant." I didn't know what better way to break the news, so I just said it. Brooke and Brianna were too busy laughing to hear me, but Kris heard what I said.

"What? You're pregnant. By who?" she asked.

"Who you think fool? Josh!" I said.

The room went silent. I started to feel uneasy, and I knew Brooke wouldn't be happy about it because of Josh's lifestyle. I didn't want to be the one to break the silence for once, so I just stood there and waited for one of them to say something. Just then, my phone started ringing. I looked at the screen and it was Josh.

"Hey baby, where are you? We need to talk," I said.

"Sorry little lady, but you won't be talking to Josh anytime soon unless we get what we want," said the guy on the other end of the phone.

"Who the fuck is this? Where is Josh?" I asked.

"He's indisposed right now. But if you ever want to see him alive again, you have Hank call this number at 9 o'clock tonight. Don't be late," he said.

Just before he hung up, I said, "Wait, let me talk to him. I just need to know he's ok." I begged.

Tears began to stream down my face as I waited in sheer panic to hear Josh's voice. I heard some muffling in the background, and it felt like an eternity before Josh got on the phone. By then, my sisters were standing around me waiting to find out what was going on.

"Hello?" he said.

"Baby, are you ok? Did they hurt you?" I asked, crying.

"Yea, I'm fine. Look, I need you to stay calm, and go tell Pops what's up. Don't worry about me, I will be fine."

Before I could say anything else, the line went dead and the call ended. I was speechless and in shock.

"What's wrong B?" asked Brooke.

"Josh has been kidnapped. I gotta go."

And with that, I ran out the house, jumped in my car and headed straight to River Hills to see Hank.

To Be Continued……..

Connect with Author Sylvannah
Facebook: Author Sylvannah
Follow her on Instagram: @sylvannahwrites

Stay connected for hot reads & updates
Facebook: Kindred Soul Publications
Join our reading group on Facebook: Kindred Soul
Readers & Authors
Tweet us on Twitter: kindredsoulpub
Follow us on Instagram: kindredsoulpublications
Visit our website:
http://kindredsoulpublications.com/

Stay up to date on new releases, contests and sneak peeks

by *texting KindredSoul to 482828*

Kindred Soul is accepting submissions in the following genres:

urban fiction, urban romance, women's fiction & Christian fiction. Submit the first 3 chapters of your completed manuscript, your contact info, and a brief bio to kindredsoulpublications@gmail.com and please allow 7-10 days for a response!

Made in the USA
San Bernardino, CA
01 October 2017